Pendleton's Penance

DEAN BARRY

PAGE PUBLISHING, INC.
New York, NY

First originally published by Page Publishing, Inc. 2015

ISBN 978-1-68213-090-2 (pbk)
ISBN 978-1-68213-091-9 (digital)

Printed in the United States of America

Episode 1

It was June 21, 1946, a drizzly day. London, England, was full swing into summer season. I was aboard the HMS *Pride*. I remember back on board ship when Pendleton was an ltd. Admiral Hornblower was a captain, and I was a war correspondent waiting for my release from the navy. The war was over, and the troops were getting restless.

To cheer them up, we gave the crew a musical show, starring the Andrews Sisters who were on tour with the USO. After they performed, we did our version of the Andrews Sisters. Well, it wasn't really the Andrews Sisters. Actually, it was me and Penny trying to be the Andrews Sisters. Hornblower was Hitler. That's right, Hitler. The opening scene was the sisters singing "Don't Sit under the Apple Tree," while they gave Hitler a spanking on his bare behind. When the show was over, I interviewed the real Andrews Sisters. I won't soon forget one answer in particular. I asked Lavern how come they enjoyed singing "Don't Sit under the Apple Tree." Her sister answered for her and said, "Because Lavern always sings 'Don't Sit under the Apple Tree' I'm horny as can be."

I broke in and asked how they liked working with Jimmy Durant. Maxine answered that they were doing a show. She was sitting on the piano, showing a lot of leg, and Jimmy was singing "Inka Dinka Doo." I looked at his crotch and sang "No, that will never do." Jimmy sang back "That's true, but my snozzola will do." The soldiers thought that it was hilarious and broke into loud laughter.

From then on, we always worked with him whenever we could. He was a lovely man.

I finished the interview, and we were about to go our separate ways when Lavern said, "Tell Pendleton that I don't like the fact that his legs are prettier than mine." We chuckled and parted.

At that time, I was known as Ash. My real name is Rex Ashley.

I presently write for London's *The Mirror*. My assignment for this Sunday's social column is to cover the queen's charity ball, which donates all the funds to the healthcare of poor children.

My story began with a special meeting at The Royal Yacht Club, the most prestigious club in all of England, meeting before their monthly dance to solicit money for the queen's annual charity ball.

The Commodore Admiral Herasio Hornblower III was in charge. He wielded a heavy gavel, I'm told. As I stood there, taking notes, the mayor of London came into the Yacht Club hall to issue a challenge to the members present.

"For the royal sum of two hundred pounds, I challenge anyone to cause the admiral to breakup during his speech," he said.

The first member to take the challenge suggested a squirting microphone be installed. The second thought that a shocking microphone would be good. The third member felt an exploding cap glued on the head of his gavel would be funny.

I remember very clearly the look on Lord Pendleton's face as he stood.

"Gentlemen," he said, "I think you're going down the path backwards. Your thoughts are immature. I herby take this challenge. I'll surprise you with the outcome."

I will never forget the arrival of the admiral. One hour late. This was unheard of for a man of his stature. He quickly organized the group and took charge.

"Gentlemen, gentlemen, to order. We were embarrassed last year with the meager financial showing of this club. We are English and proud. We are frugal but not cheap. I need not remind you that we have a royal charter dating back three hundred years. The queen, I must say, can revoke it at any time."

The hall was silent, but a murmur was heard rumbling through. One man stood. "Admiral," he yelled, "your fly is open."

I watched the admiral reach down to zip up his fly. He suddenly realized that the members of the club were breaking his marbles. He didn't seemed concerned at the moment, but his attempt to gain order caused him to slam his gavel against the podium. The gavel exploded with a very loud bang, spreading smoke and dust all over him. The admiral stepped back and gazed at the crowd, his face red with embarrassment. I laughed as hard as anyone else in the room, even though I did like the man.

It didn't take long for the admiral to regain his composure.

"I am asking each of you to donate five hundred pounds this year. We will make up for the drought last year. That's right, blokes, five hundred pounds per head."

It seemed that the admiral had things under control when another member stood and requested that the first dance of tonight's ball be the chicken dance.

"What the bloody hell is the chicken dance?" the admiral replied.

"It's the same as the electric slide," the member answered.

The admiral was getting a bit perplexed but kept a stiff upper lip.

"I say," the admiral boomed, "it's getting rather hot in here. Would one of you so-called gentlemen turn on the fans?" He then turned to the man suggesting the crazy dances and asked, "What the hell is the electric slide?"

He was near the end of his speech, and each of us waited for Pendleton's trick to happen. We knew it had to be more than the exploding gavel.

Another member injected, "It's a line dance just like the hokey pokey."

The admiral gave up and started to brush his podium off. He looked up at the overhead fan and started to sneeze.

"The hell with it." He sneezed again. "Let's do the Macarena. That's one I am good at."

His face was contorted to sneeze again, and then he started scratching his ear his nose and his hands.

The members, in the know, were rolling in laughter. I felt sorry for the old boy even though it was funny. I was taking notes for my column and noticed Lord Pendleton and his latest squeeze, Deana, entering as the admiral, still sneezing, ended his speech. It was obvious that the admiral had quickly figured out it was Pendleton who caused all this trouble.

"Pendleton, old chap!" he yelled. "So good to see you could make it. Each of the members has pledged one thousand pounds to the queen's charity this year. You will also, I assume?"

Lord Pendleton, caught completely off guard, was speechless. Deana, however, was not. She answered for him. "Yes, of course. Lord Pendleton is in," she said, very assured.

I watch as Lord Pendleton almost had a heart attack. His glance hit me full on. He then turned to the podium.

"Deana, are you crazy?" he quickly replied. "Admiral Hornblower, I-I-I am not—" he stuttered, as the admiral cut him off before he could complete the statement.

"Thank you, Lord Pendleton," the admiral replied, "for your very generous donation. I was just kidding about the amount. The rest of us only entered five hundred pounds each, but I'm sure, old man, that the queen will be happy with you."

I watched as the room exploded into laughter. I could see Pendleton's red panties showing through his white uniform. He was not well liked by most due to his pompous nature. I personally think he is worse than the all the rest put together, and they were all pretty bad. Deana noticed his red panties also.

"Penny," she said, "I'm getting turned on by your undies. You should be more careful in your selection of colors."

At this time, the admiral interceded.

"Perhaps," he said, "you and Her Majesty, the queen, can have a secret get together to celebrate this momentous donation."

I felt bad for Pendleton as the other members roared with laughter again. Deana was embarrassed by her giddy intervention in Pendleton's affairs. Pendleton was angry.

"Deana," he yelled loudly, "I hope you never again speak for me without my permission."

Deana, an ex-model and perpetual beauty, absolutely tall and slender, the proverbial knockout, had a résumé a mile long—Holliston, Revlon, Boston bride, Calvin Kline, Armani. She screamed for male eyes only and could work a room just by entering. The admiral noticed her as well as every other guy in the place. He looked right by Pendleton as he spoke to her.

"Deana," said the admiral, "we always look forward to seeing you. You are beautiful tonight. Would you do me the honor of the first dance?"

She glanced at Pendleton for the okay. Pendleton nodded approval. Pendleton then asked if it would be the chicken dance or the hokey pokey. The admiral tried to smile but was not amused.

After the first dance, Deana returned to Pendleton's side to hang on his arm as his trophy date. "Penny, he ask me to go to bed with him. What shall I say, dear?"

"I would like you to oblige him. Make sure you introduce him to our best friend, Willy. Bring the cell phone with you. I need a good laugh."

"Penny, are you sure I should introduce him to Willy?"

"Of course you should. Tell him he can pet it. It won't bite. Take some pictures so I can embarrass him at the club. He is so pompous, I can't stand him. I think everyone in the club feels that way also."

"Alright, honey, I'll see what he has under there. Wish me luck."

"He's the one that is going to need luck. When I get through with him, he will be crying in his beer."

The admiral walked by, and Deana felt it was time to act. "Ohhh, Admiral, I need to talk to you."

"Yes, my dear, what is it."

"Is there some place where we can be alone?"

"Yes, dear, follow me."

The admiral led her to the commodore's lodge. A room he has at his disposal, which comes with his position as commodore. Little did he know that a dice game was in progress in the room next door.

"Deana, we can talk in here," he whispered.

"Commodore, this is beautiful. What a nice room. It's so well decorated. Look at the pretty colors. We can have some randy fun here, don't you think so?

"Deana, my dear, right now, the only color I want to see is the color of your smooth soft pink boobs. Which I believe Pendleton calls Ursula and Christina."

"Why, Commodore, I think you are chatting me up. Did Penny actually talk about my figure?"

"Well, yes, he talked about you, Deana. I think you should be happy to be so beautiful. I personally think that you are the only real one around here."

The dice game in the next room was getting interesting due to the fact the queen had just arrived. Her first action was to change the set of dice to her own royal set. As she looked at the American ambassador, she whipped off her hoop skirt, handed him the dice, and said, "Here, rub them on my ass for good luck. Does that holy roller boss of yours play dice?"

"No, Your Majesty," answered the ambassador. "The president is too busy waging war on the gays."

******

Meanwhile, back in the commodore's locker.

"Admiral, I can only get it on in the dark. We will have to turn off the lights."

"Oh yes, that will be fine with me. Go ahead, turn them off."

She killed the lights, then helped him disrobe. While they jockeyed for position, she fumbled for the cell phone somewhere on the floor. Her first attempt came up with a shoe. The next was her bra. She felt around his body to give him a thrill, so his mind would stay tuned in. He sighed, then groaned. Deana smiled to herself, then reached for the camera again.

"Where the hell is it?" she said loud enough for him to hear.

"It's between my legs," he anxiously announced. "Don't you know what a man looks like?"

She rubbed her silky smooth breast against his chest to keep him interested. "Of course I know what men look like," she replied. "Believe me, I truly know your bloody brain is between your legs. I will be right back. Don't move."

"Where the blooming hell are you going?"

"The bathroom. Maybe you want to watch. I know you sailors like it wet and wild."

"No, thanks, if I get up now, I'll lose everything. Hurry back."

Deana wanted to find her cell phone camera but couldn't tell him, of course. After a while, she returned, still without the camera.

"I'm back, dear. Did you miss me?"

"Of course I missed you. My bloody thing went dead while you were fooling around."

"I was only gone for ten seconds. Don't worry, I'll fix it for you. Little boys like you often need a spanking. Like Prince Charles, you seem to have a problem staying on top of things. Him with his horses, and you with your absent-minded little bad boy."

"Hurry, you bloody wench, I can't wait forever."

"Yes I'm going as fast as I can," Deana whispered.

"Hurry, I'm coming. I'm coming. Hurry."

"How did this happen, Admiral? I haven't done anything yet. Don't you have any control for the love of the queen."

"Sorry, Deana my dear, but it's all over. You missed all the fun. I wanted to show you a good time, but oftentimes, I have a quick release."

"That's okay, Commodore. I'm used to that. Penny does that all the time."

The get-together was over. She excused herself and headed for the bathroom, her clothing in hand.

At the exact moment she closed the bathroom door, she heard a woman's voice accompanied by a loud banging upon the commodore's door. It seems that the queen who was playing dice next door needed to use the bathroom.

"Open this door in the name of the queen," she yelled. "Do you hear me, you bloody buffoon. I need to pee. Quickly open this door." She waited an instant, then asked, "Herasio, are you in there?"

The admiral was now in a panic. Little did he know, it was about to get a lot worse. He heard the queen talking to another female, then much more intense banging on the door. To him, it seemed like being at war on his ship.

"Pendleton told me I could find you here," the second voice shouted.

"No, dear, I'm not here . . . I mean, don't come in yet. I am in the bathroom, and the door is open."

"Oh, the door is open." She had misunderstood. He meant the bathroom door. She thought the commodore's room door.

"I'm coming in," she whispered in a very, very stern voice.

The heavy door squeaked as it pivoted on its hinges, then slammed open against the wall. Mrs. Hornblower, standing behind the queen, just stood there, looking at Mr. Hornblower. He was standing in the nude facing them, very embarrassed. The bathroom door opened, and there stood Deana, also facing them and also completely nude.

"My god!" screamed Mrs. Hornblower. "You're gay."

"My god!" screamed the queen. "You're fat."

Mr. Hornblower looked at Deana to see what his wife was talking about. Deana stood in the bathroom door, silhouetted by the bathroom light. Her penis hung down about six inches.

"God save the queen," he yelled, then looked back to his wife of forty years.

Deana closed the door to finish getting dressed. The wife turned to leave, then yelled, "If you go down like a submarine, I will go down in luxury. To keep my mouth closed and our marriage together, I'll expect compensation in the form of two mink coats and new gold Jaguar delivered by the day after tomorrow. I believe the correct submarine time will be oh thirteen hundred."

The queen entered the room and headed for the bathroom.

"Well, my good man, you now are obligated to me also. You can count on me not to tell everyone about your gay encounter. I will expect you in my quarters in one hour after I kick ass in the card room."

When she got to the bathroom, Deana was already dressed. The queen eyed her up and down, then smiled. "Who the bloody hell would ever have thought that you were a transsexual? If you expect me to keep your secret, then you will be in my quarters in two hours from now."

Deana smiled widely, then replied to the queen's demand. "Your Majesty," she whispered with a giggle, "I really don't care if you keep my secret, but I will be in your room as ordered."

Mrs. Hornblower then slammed the door and turned to leave, bumping into Pendleton on her way out.

"Thank you, my lord, for the information. I really do believe all you lads are perverted pigs."

Deana winked at the queen now on the throne, then exited the room to find Pendleton waiting for her.

"Did he see wee Willy dear?" Pendleton asked.

"No, he climaxed prematurely. What a dickhead. I can't believe he is just like you. Pompous and premature, do all you Yacht Club people go to the school for little boys? I have to go find a guy that can keep up with me."

"Did you get any pictures of his thing?"

"I couldn't find the cell phone. It rolled under the bed. I'll have to go back later to get it."

"How the hell am I going to embarrass him?"

"Maybe you can hold his hand in public or tell him I'm a trans-sexual. That should do it. Then start a rumor in the club before his wife does."

Pendleton smirked. "What do you mean his wife?"

"His wife saw me in the nude!"

"I know, I sent her in to catch him." He laughed and continued talking. "I didn't think it would be this good, but it would have been better to put a picture up on the bulletin board. Never mind, we have to go now.""Penny, he told me he is going to get me invited to the queen's ball even if you have to come along also.

"Really, dear, that will be great. I can get close to the queen and enhance my future. Do you think the admiral thinks it was an accident that his wife found him with you?"

"I don't think he heard the wife say you sent him as she opened the door. If he did, he would kill you."

******

I was working on my column for the queen's ball when it was brought to my attention that the Yacht Club was planning a tall ship parade to the Caribbean, then the States to raise funds. I realized I only had until tonight to get myself ready to attend. I went to the hall to see the preparations and found the admiral and the queen together.

The royal hall was active. Admiral Herasio Hornblower III was in the queen's chambers gossiping with his dear friend, Her Majesty, Elisabeth, Queen of England.

She was a gossip crackhead and a royal cut-up and was sponsoring this charity ball. She needed her fix of gossip.

The admiral is excited about his big donation.

"Your Majesty," he whispered, "before the ball gets underway, I have some great news for you. We raised a lot of money this year. You'll never guess who the largest donor is."

"Spare me the guessing game, Admiral. Who is it?"

"It's that annoyance to the crown, Pendleton."

The queen glanced at him, not believing.

"Pendleton, that pompous picture of puck, gave the most! I don't believe it. Are you sure?"

"Yes, Your Majesty, he did. I hope you can see fit to allow me to invite him and his friend Deana to your charity ball?"

"Nonsense, Admiral. You know that your entire club is welcome here tonight. Even if it includes that pompous Pendleton trying to buy his way in. Even that nasty American shock joke Howard Stem has more class than Pendleton. If Lord Pendleton wasn't a war hero, he would be just a commoner. Even Boy George has more balls and is more loyal to the crown."

The admiral interjected. "I'm not too sure either of them has any balls."

The queen chuckled and replied, "I'll have to take a royal look during our Halloween party."

The admiral excused himself to go find Pendleton who was already at the ball. Deana, his steady girlfriend whom he enjoys showing off, accompanies him.

The queen stayed behind to watch her favorite American program *Orange County Choppers*. She enjoys watching the father interfere and slow things down.

I watched the admiral leave the queen's quarters. I decided to follow him to get some inside information for his column. The admiral met up with Pendleton and Deana. Pendleton, a suave man, was charming all the ladies with his dancing. His ex-navy buddy Niles Pishposs the schemer was chatting him up about the royal family.

******

"I say Pendleton. Prince Phillip is giving all the ladies the eye."

"Aye, mate, do you think the prince sniffs around?"

"I'm quite sure he does. His tongue is so long, it hits his knees. I wonder, Penny old chap, what the prince would look like in heels."

"Excuse me, Niles, did you ask if he licks or sniffs around."

"I've heard that he likes to suck toes," replied Pendleton.

Niles stopped to think, then said, "So does the Duchess of York. The Brits are into sucking toes, and the Yanks are into sucking genitals. Either way, you get hair in your mouth, ay what, Penny old boy. It's rumored that he looks prettier in a dress than the queen. Everyone knows she wears the pants and does the spanking. We know who is Greek in that family, and he isn't touching her ass."

Niles smiled. "The old girl's fashion sense is not up-to-date. Is it, old boy?"

Pendleton was laughing full volume.

"Yes, early K Mart I believe," he coughed out.

Niles chuckled. "The Yanks call it Goodwill fashions because all the drag queens shop there. I believe it is only right that the queen looks the same. Do you think she is still a virgin?"

"Sorry, old boy, I won't enter that area. Not my business, what."

"Pendleton, I understand that all the American queens wear two pairs of nylons to hide hairy legs, but our queen wears none because Prince Phillip likes hairy legs."

"Penny, is it true that the prince is a Greek?"

"Yes, Niles. His heritage was always interested in hairy legs."

******

The queen was working the crowd. She was out to get promises of money to help the charity and would use any information she could get. Armed with information from Rex Ashley regarding the conversation between Pendleton and Niles, she happened upon the two men in conversation.

Standing behind them, she recalled the information obtained from Rex. She bit her tongue, then responded. "Disrespect, Pendleton," she uttered in a very loud but dignified voice. "How can a man be so much like Errol Flynn but act so much like Cheech and Chong?" The queen stopped to look at Niles. "Who is this commoner?"

The two men, caught completely off guard, were embarrassed. Pendleton and his navy buddy Niles were speechless.

"His . . . His name is Niles Pishposs, Your Majesty."

The queen is flustered.

"You're a fool, and he is nothing but a commoner who will be ejected."

She turned quickly, then scurried away totally upset.

"I say, Niles old boy, what the hell brought her on? Let's head for the bar before the old girl has us tossed out."

******

Standing at the bar talking, Pendleton and Niles enjoyed drinks.

"Pendleton old boy, I am trying to buy the yacht from a friend of the admirals. His name is Captain Coldpepper. He wants too much money for it. I have some embarrassing pictures of Admiral Hornblower that I would prefer you to show him, so he can influence his friend Coldpepper to drop the price.

"Good show, old man," replied Pendleton. "You will have to show the pictures yourself. I have enough trouble in my life at the moment."

Pendleton and Niles spent the evening, drinking together accompanied by Deana. They ended the perfect evening walking in the queen's private garden together.

Meanwhile, the admiral and the queen are conversing again.

"Your Majesty, Pendleton has arrived. He is accompanied by his commoner friend, Niles. I don't like either of them, but at least, Pendleton has an invitation."

"Yes, Admiral, I have met Niles. He is a squint of a man I wouldn't even wish him on Ireland.

Have him removed. He is arrogant, not fit for a royal occasion."

"With pleasure, I will, Your Majesty."

******

I could recall the Royal Guard hunting for Niles. They looked everywhere, except the queen's garden. The queen had a strong distaste for him and was even less happy with Pendleton. The guard had been ordered to give Niles a royal talking to, then toss him out on his ass. I remember this quite vividly because it was so unusual for a commoner to be in the castle and just as unusual to see the guards toss someone out. The captain of the guard actually told Niles that he was Irish dirt compared to himself being from the order of Orange.

******

It was an unusually warm evening. The queen's garden was in full bloom. Pendleton, Deana, and Niles were enjoying nature at its best. They decided to wager on the ability of one of them to fill a beer bottle with pee. The one who came closest to the top would be the winner. It would be a race between them performed one at a time.

I remember the scene clearly. Pendleton went first. He had a long, very slender penis. His friends called him Needle Dick. He virtually injected the bottle and only filled it one-third full. Next came Niles he was so drunk, he peed on his hand and just barely wet the bottom of the bottle.

Now came Deana, she filled the bottle to overflowing. This, in itself, was no mean feat, but what followed was hilarious. I remember this quite clearly. I was hiding in the next row of flowers looking for information for my column. The dialogue that followed was real. I couldn't wait to tell the queen all that I knew, but it had to wait. I wasn't about to miss out on the best part of the evening.

******

"Pendleton old man, stop. I need to deposit some of this liquor."

Niles then pulled his zipper down deftly, exposing his blade. "Look, old man, I'm going to water the old girl's roses."

Pendleton, now holding onto a tree to remain in the upright position, was folded over laughing.

"Niles, might I challenge you to a contest?"

"Jolly good," replied Niles, his voice slurred from liquor.

Deana was drunk also. "Niles, I have to pee too," she said.

At this time, Pendleton, who was finishing his last beer for the evening, held the empty bottle up and said, "This is the challenge, folks. Whoever fills the bottle closest to the top is the blooming winner."

"I want to play too," cried Deana.

"Deana," Niles replied, "you're a girl. How are you going to pee in a bottle without making a mess?"

She leaned against Niles while she pulled her undies down.

"My god," Niles said, "what the bloody hell is that?"

"That's my wee Willy winker," she replied.

"You have a dick, old girl, what!"

"Yes, dear. Nice, isn't it?"

"Pendleton, she has a dick. Did you know that?"

"Yes, I love it. We have a lot of fun with it. I say," he slurred, "would you like to try it?"

"Yes Niles," Deana whispered. "Why don't you try it? I'll show you what a proper lady can do."

Niles replied, "No, thank you. Pink elephants are enough for me. Pink dickeys are out of the question, you bloody freak.

Pendleton, now standing upright, told the other two he will go first in the bottle contest. "Penny, old chap," Niles interjected, "you haven't even covered the bottom of the bottle. Where did you get that penis? It the skinniest thing I've ever seen. We will have to call you Needle Dick from now on. It's my turn, and I know I can beat you two."

Niles filled the bottle halfway up and was happy to see such a good amount. He was sure he'd win the contest.

"Niles, I must tell you, my friend, your shoes are getting watered also."

Deana whispered, "Niles, you didn't do much better than Pendleton. I can beat that easily."

"Deana, I doubt you can beat Niles," replied Pendleton.

"Well, if I do, what will you give me?"

"I'll give you a bouquet of flowers of unmatched beauty straight from the queen's best roses."

"You're on, Penny," Deana answered. "I'll fill this up quickly. I haven't peed in a few hours."

"Look, Niles, you lose! The bottle is overflowing." Pendleton laughed.

Niles had become so focused on Deana's extra body part, he lost grip of the tree and fell into the rose bed, taking Deana along with him. The bottle of pee popped into the air and sprayed both of them.

Pendleton tried to catch the bottle but leaned over to far and joined them in the thorn bush.

******

I remember the scene vividly. I thought the three of them were fools of the biggest kind.

They say I smoke too much grass, but I've never done anything like that.

They were drunk but could still feel the thorns. Deana was screaming, and Niles was cursing so loud, they woke up the queen's gardener.

He heard the commotion through his cottage window and released the hounds. He then ran out to see Deana and Niles thrashing about in the rose garden.

The biggest dog jumped on Niles and bit him. Niles promptly bit the dog back. The dog smelled the spilled urine, lifted his leg, and peed on Niles and Deana.

The other dog jumped on Pendleton and started ferociously licking his face. Every time Pendleton cried out for help, the dog's massive tongue went in his mouth. He spat it out, but the dog got him again.

Deana looked over. "Penny," she said, "I know the dog French kissing you first, but you look like you're enjoying it too much. If this keeps up, I'm going to look for a new boyfriend." She stopped then added, "Make sure you gargle in the morning, dear."

I felt bad for them, so I went around the bushes and extended my hand. Unfortunately, Deana and Niles grabbed me at the same time. The third dog jumped on my back, and I became one more blooming victim. I was pushed into the rose bed and got tangled up in the thorns. Luckily, I landed on Deana. Her dress was up, and her panties were still down. I slowly positioned myself to take full advantage of the situation. My hand felt her beautiful body parts. The rest of my body was being tortured by the thorns. I had misery and delight at the same time. God works in strange ways, I told myself.

The gamer appeared and called of the dogs. He helped us one by one. Thinking Deana was a lady in distress, he pulled her out of the bushes first, then gave her a very strange look.

The next morning, I addressed the queen. I told her that Niles and Pendleton were the ones who ruined her flowerbeds. I intentionally left Deana out of it, and of course, I didn't squeal on myself.

The queen was furious. She called Pendleton and the gang in front of her that evening. Pendleton came dressed in his best outfit. He was happy and smiling, thinking she would award him for helping with the charity ball.

She addressed Deana first, asking her what had happened in the garden last evening with the two school-like children. Deana told her she saw Niles peeing on the flowers when a big dog jumped on him. He bit the dog as I tried to stop him. She went on to say that Pendleton was there also, but she thought he was innocent.

The queen thanked her, then told her she was in the company of scoundrels. She was not a very good liar, and she should chose her friends more carefully, then excused her.

The next one to feel the wrath of the queen was Pendleton. The queen scowled at the sight of him.

"Your knighthood is revoked," she yelled. "Furthermore, all your loans are hereby recalled by the crown."

She then stood full of fury. "I am not enjoying your insolent behavior."

Pendleton was shocked. He wasn't sure why this was happening.

"Your Majesty, I don't understand. What did I do to deserve this?"

The queen told him she knew that he peed on her prize flowers. "I didn't pee on your flowers . . . It was Niles the commoner."

"Well, you should have stopped him especially that he is a commoner you brought into my home. My thirty-five-thousand-pound prize rose is dead. If this were the old days, your head would be lying on the floor right beside his. Pendleton, you will have to work diligently to ever have a chance to get your knighthood back. You have acted like a child. I didn't expect this from a naval reserve captain. Let alone a lord. Leave me this moment, you fool."

******

I remember the gossip around the town and the Yacht Club. Pendleton was humiliated and shunned. The club members were happy not to have to put up with him. Penny called a family meeting to plan his comeback. He told me later that Deana, Iris, and Cornelius Quackenbush, the butler, tried to help him.

******

"I will turn my ship into a bed and breakfast in the States," he blurted out to no one in particular. "Deana, do you remember when we met. You were a social director on the cruise ship, and I was your passenger. We danced all night, and now we are here. It takes an elegant person to direct people to the right place in life. I have to ask a favor of you, Deana. Would you be a darling and be my social director when we get to the States?"

"I don't understand," Deana said. "Why, what happened?"

"The queen has denounced me because of you and Niles who also fell on her flowers."

"Oh, I'm so sorry to hear that. Why do we have to go to the States?"

"I'm ruined here. I am broke except for my yacht."

Deana is shocked. "You must have done something else besides that."

"No," he said. "I'm unsure what transpired, but I am heading for the States. First New York, then Key West for the winter. Thank God, it's summer. Now we can make it across the pond in safety."

At this point, the butler spoke up. "Sir," he said, "I served in WWII on that magnificent *Queen Mary* as a steward. I will not cross the Atlantic ocean in that swamp buggy of yours. Perhaps I'll join you at a later date."

Iris let it be known that she was present. "Cornelius," she whispered, "you can be my servant."

Deana reflected on the problem for a moment, then asked, "How will we pay for food and fuel?"

"I will sell my estate to pay the queen. The rest will get us across to Manhattan, plus I will make Niles chip in to pay for his stupidity."

"Sir, when you get to America, send for me. I will join you if need be," replied Cornelius.

******

They have arrived at the marina in New York after an uneventful trip across the Atlantic. Docked next to the aircraft carrier Intrepid.

"I like this boat slip," Pendleton said to Deana. "Look at the view. "We can put a sign up on our roof to get customers from the tour groups on that aircraft carrier." He paused to look around, stopping at his friend Deana.

"Deana, we need some crew to help us operate the B&B. I have placed an ad in the local paper for a steward and a cook."

"Great," Deana replied. "We are already in business. We can start making money very soon."

"Yes, dear, we will interview and select a crew this week."

Deana was happy and anxious to proceed.

"Penny, would you like to tour the carrier with me?"

"No, dear, I have seen enough aircraft carriers in my life."

"Okay. I'll go alone."

******

The ad in the paper brought in only a couple of calls, giving them few workers to choose from.

The first interview was for a steward but no men show up, just one Southern belle named Billie Joe May.

It was Deana's job to interview first. She was ready with what she thought were the right questions.

"Billie, how are you?" Deana asked. "Tell me about yourself."

"Well," Billie replied, "I learned all my skills in flight attendant school. I enjoy working with people. I'm strong enough to help with the boat chores, and I need a means to travel. That's why I became a stewardess."

"Great, Billie, you're hired. When can you start?"

Deana was excited by Billie who was very pretty with a bubbly personality and looked very strong. Pendleton liked her looks also, but he won't show it in front of Deana.

The next interview was for the cook's position. A sweet old lady of about eighty years, looking for excitement and travel, gave it a try.

"Hi, Mr. Captain." She winked, then asked, "How are you, sweetie?"

Lord Pendleton smiled at the thought of her flirting with him, a man so much above her post in life.

"You have a great résumé. It is somewhat outdated, madam."

"Of course it is. I haven't had to work for a long time. My husband just kicked the bucket, and now I'm on the hunt for a new man." She winked at him again, then smiled.

"I'm sorry to hear that," interceded Deana. "When did he pass away?"

"Yesterday morning. I don't have time to fool around. I'm eighty-two and horny as hell." She yawned, then quickly fell asleep.

Next came the Elvis lookalike.

"Well, Elvis," asked the captain, "why do you want to cook on board a yacht?"

"Yes, Captain, I would be happy to answer that question ya'll," he replied in his best Southern drawl. "I love to make American food. I'm especially good at hot dogs and burgers and peanut butter sandwiches." He paused to get the captain's reaction, then continued, "Ms. Deana, you sure are a fine-looking lady. I might have to leave the boat now and then to perform. Will that be all right, Captain?"

"Sure, Mr. Presley."

"Captain, I know a heck of a lot of jokes. Ya'll want to hear one?"

"Elvis," interceded the captain, anxious to get rid of the singer, "we will call you if we can get a sighting."

The Elvis lookalike was shown the door.

"Billie, send in the next one," shouted Deana.

Billie shouted back, "You two had better come see this."

They arrived at the companion way ladder and stopped, amazed at the sight.

"What the hell is this?" Deana whispered to Pendleton.

"It's a real pirate." Billie Joe giggled.

"I'm goddamn stuck," slurred the pirate. "My wooden peg leg is between the boat and the boarding ramp."

"He's bloody stuck!" exclaimed the captain.

The pirate's ferret on his left shoulder was all a flutter. His parrot, named Maxi, on his right started to swear, then looked at

Pendleton and said in a very clear Jewish accent, "Flagella, look at the pretty shoes. Goddamn!" The pirate's eye patch was now in the middle of his head, covering his nose. "You do look like a faggot. Now help me get lose, ya goddamn sissy."

He tossed his empty whiskey bottle over his shoulder aimed at the water but missed and broke a window on the yacht next door.

"What the hell is going on over there?" yelled the owner.

The parrot spoke again. "Screw you, dickhead," he squawked.

José, a serene little Pekingese and ship's mascot, finally arrived on the scene. He looked at the pirate that funny way he has, slowly advancing toward him as stealthily as could. He pranced around him twice while he decided what to do about the dirty pirate. He finally looked up at the love boats and things near the sea.

She paused. "Look at that big aircraft carrier. I love that too."

"What can you cook?" asked Billie Joe.

"I am chef. I cook all things," replied Olga, with a Russian accent that Deana could barely understand. The interview lasted a while. During the time, Olga declared that she cooked for Gorbachev and Yelson and the KBG. Her food was loved by the prisoners on death row.

"I even cooked in the Gulag, but it didn't count."

"Why didn't it count?" asked Deana.

"The pigs would eat yellow snow. They would eat frozen horse. They would eat dead rats, yeah! Of course they thought my food was good."

Deana chose Olga, thinking she was big enough to be able to help on board with landing the boat and other chores including cooking.

******

The captain addressed Billie Joe, Olga, and Deana. "Now I have to tell you that we are just starting up. I don't have enough money to pay you. I will sign a contract to give you back pay when we get to Key West. In the meantime, we will all work for room and board."

Both ladies agreed and moved on board the yacht that day.

When Olga was introduced to the kitchen, she looked bewildered. Olga doesn't know how to operate the ship's equipment, so she stalls to figure things out.

"I have to get some special groceries," she said, "and I need rubbles and a ride."

"Billie Joe will you take you," replied Deana, "to the store in a cab and help you shop."

"Olga, where are you from?" asked Billie Joe.

"Russia. We need to go to little Odessa to shop. There I can speak Russian and get what we need." She then asked Billie what she was all about. "I was an airline flight attendant. I got laid off after the airline shut down."

"Yeah, I fly too," added Olga.

******

After their shopping trip, they returned to the yacht, loaded down with groceries. Olga was ready to cook a fish. She had some pickles and bread to go with it.

"I will fry the fish and put chocolaty covering on it. This is for us. We don't get paid, so they get fish stew. We get the good stuff."

She made a stew from the fish head and potatoes, then threw in the pickles. She brought the dish up stairs to Pendleton and Deana.

"This is special meal. Even Gorbachev likes it." She smiled.

The captain and Deana smiled back and tasted it. They both reacted at the same time. Totally disgusted, they placed their plates on the floor so José would eat it.

José quickly ran, expecting a good meal, and sniffed it, gave them a funny look, then walked away with his tail down as though he was mad at them.

Olga was still smiling at them waiting for their oohs and aahs.

The captain excused Olga and turned to Deana. "We can't use Olga for a cook. This is awful."

"Yes, dear, but she will make a great deck hand until we find someone who can cook better. I'll talk with her and tell her that we only eat vegetables, salad, and chicken. Nobody can screw that up."

Parrot then started to chew on the man's wooden leg. "Get away, filthy swine," hissed the pirate.

"Get away, filthy swine," squawked the parrot.

The pirate tried to kick him. José dodged the kick with ease, smiled, then pirouetted on his hind legs, and at the same instant, managed to pee on the pirate's good leg instead.

The pirate kicked at him again. His wooden leg, still jammed in the dock, cracked, sounding like a twig in the woods. Disconnected instantly from the dock, his left leg six inches shorter, he lost his balance and fell overboard into the water with a loud wet splash.

The ferret, making all sorts of noise, jumped in an effort to stay dry. He landed on the rail, then jumped down to the deck where him and José met nose to nose. They both looked over the side to see where the pirate was, then looked at each other and smiled. Meanwhile, the parrot landed on the ship's railing, looked over the side, and very loudly squawked, "Schmuck, schmuck, schmuck." Then it flew up to the edge of the main cabin.

"Grab that stinking bloke!" yelled the captain, as he reached toward the man.

"He's in the water!" screamed Billie Joe, as she jumped overboard.

"I'll save him," replied the captain, running down the gang-plank to fish him out.

"You bloody bastards," gurgled the pirate, looking up at José and the ferret.

"You bloody bastard," cried the parrot from up high, looking down at the pirate.

The captain, kneeling on the dock with his hand out to help the pirate, was pulled in by the pirate instead.

"Aye, mate," yelled the pirate, "you are a sissy man, aren't you."

"I'll get help," yelled Deana as she ran inside. "Here we come," she called out, suddenly appearing with Olga who was mumbling something in Russian.

"I will pull for you to come out," Olga said as she reached down and pulled out each one as though they were as light as balsa wood.

They brought the pirate inside to help him dry off. Pendleton, insensitive as usual, ordered him not to rip anything with his jagged wooden stump. The pirate looked at him disdainfully.

"Aye, mate, you are lucky if I don't sue. You blooming land lubber." They got the pirate dried off and gave him a shot of whiskey.

He grabbed the whole bottle and started guzzling. The parrot, ferret, and José followed them into the boat.

The rat-looking pirate constantly adjusted his eye patch and finally zeroed in on the girls.

"Aye, missy, you're a pretty one, you are."

The parrot flew all around the room twice and landed on the pirate's right shoulder. "Fungue, fungue, fungue," he said three times, then started laughing.

"I like you so much," slurred the pirate, "that I've decided to show you what's under the patch." Raising the patch and revealing his empty eye socket, he turned around so everyone could view it. "Aye, missy." He smiled. "Lookie here."

"That's disgusting," cried Billie Joe.

"That's disgusting!" squawked the parrot.

"Shut up, you stupid bird," she replied.

"Shut up, you stupid whore," the bird returned.

The pirate laughed and took another swig from the bottle.

"Aye missy,"—he burped—"you might be wanting to stick your pretty little finger in the empty socket hole, mightin ya?"

The ferret, trying to get back on the pirate's shoulder, jumped and missed, landing on the dog. José started chasing the ferret, knocking over a valuable lamp, which fell against the television and broke the screen. Glass went everywhere.

"What the blooming hell!" hissed Pendleton.

"What the blooming hell!" called the parrot.

Billie Joe, busy gluing the wooden leg back together, jumped back. The pirate stood up, and his leg broke again.

"Goddamn, missy, your glue has come undone," he slurred. He then fell back onto the couch, grabbing for Billie Joe, and she landed on top of him.

"Goddamn, whore, the glue broke," squawked the parrot.

"Now this is gett'n' to be fun, missy," the pirate slurred.

"God, your breath is awful," she yelled.

Pendleton pulled her up by the arm and said, "Billie, if you need a guy that bad, put an ad in the papers."

She glared at the captain and left the room. Deana put her people skills to work, finally taking control of the scene.

"So, Mr. Pirate," she said, "I think it's time for our interview to end. We will call you in the morning if you are selected. You may keep the bottle, but you have to go ashore now."

"Aye, missy, you're a beauty, you are. We could date, couldn't we?"

The parrot squawked loudly, "We can date, whore."

Pendleton was moving toward the man to toss him out. As the pirate staggered to the door, he took another swig of whisky. The glue on the leg had not set. Again, it broke, and he rolled down the ramp, head over heels. The ferret jumped to safety, sliding down the companion way rail to the dock, meeting up with the pirate.

The parrot said, "I'm staying on this nice yacht," then flew back inside the boat and landed on Pendleton's new jacket.

The pirate looked at the parrot and said, "You filthy flying rat, I'll be back for you," then hobbled away as he continued to curse the parrot for deserting him.

Deana, in awe of what just transpired, addressed Pendleton.

"What paper did you put that ad in?"

"*The Varity*. It was cheap. Why do you ask?"

"That's an actor's paper. They use it to find work. No wonder we are getting all these crazy people. Let's finish the interviews. I've had enough for one day."

Then came Olga, the Russian lady. A giant of a person speaking broken English and claiming she was an excellent chef.

"Not much to choose from," remarked the captain.

"Except for Andre, the blooming giant."

Deana took over the interview. "Hi, Olga. Why do you think you will like living on a yacht?"

Olga walked on the broken television glass, making a crunchy sound and sat down on the couch.

"I have always been around ships at the seaport in Russia. I worked on the vessel *Laskya*."

"Okay, we will use the lady until we find someone better, but I want a sample of her salad." Deana called Olga on the intercom and told her to make two salads. The salads arrived after about an hour. The captain went first. Before he is through his first bite, they looked at each other with a strange look on their faces and simultaneously said, "Cabbage."

"My god," Deana announced, "she used cabbage instead of lettuce."

The captain spat out the cabbage and cried, "She used chili peppers instead of tomatoes."

The parrot landed on his shoulder and said, "What did you expect, Mary? She's a dumb Russian."

Deana, reaching for a glass of water, replied, "I know." Deana guzzled her water. "This parrot is smart, Penny. I'm going to find out just how smart he is." She picked a pepper from the salad. "Maxi, how would you like this nice shiny tomato?"

"No, thanks," replied the parrot.

"Are you sure?" asked Deana.

The parrot squawked loudly and said, "You have a hot ass bitch, but you aren't going make mine that way."

Pendleton, laughing, stood up and ran to the sink, then the refrigerator to grab some bread in an effort to squelch the flames in his mouth.

Deana grumbled, "Pendleton we can't use her. She's brutal. No wonder Yelson drank so much vodka. He had to put out the flames. I'll find someone soon, but until then, she will have to be the cook."

******

The next morning, Olga came up on deck. José, thinking she was a man, sneaked up on her and peed on her size 14 basketball sneaker. You might ask why he did that. The answer was that he doesn't like men. He just stopped peeing on Pendleton because Maxi told him that Penny is a Mary. José, of course, thought that meant he was a girl.

Olga chased José with a broom, screaming, "I'll put you in the soup, you little shit."

Rocco and Andres, two dock workers, were watching and getting a kick out of the new arrivals.

Olga was trying to kill José for peeing on her. She finally cornered him and picked him up by the tail, then dangled him over the railing. José was a quick thinker. He made friends by kissing her on the cheek, then he chuckled and grinned. He started thinking, *She thinks she has me by the tail, but now she is mine.*

Rocco yelled, "Look at the size of her! She must have eighteen-inch arms, and her legs are huge."

Andy jumped on board to save José. "Hey, leave him alone!" he yelled.

Olga looked at Andy, then picked him up by his collar. "Oh, look, two nice puppy dogs. I'll keep both of them," she whispered.

The captain, hearing the commotion, came on deck. His uniform, spit and polish as usual. The parrot Maxi flew out right behind him.

Pendleton hollered, "What the blooming hell is going on here?"

The parrot said, "They're fighting, numb nuts."

Rocco and Andy couldn't believe their eyes and started laughing at Pendleton and the parrot. Rocco laughed, "What a mush he is. Just like the Yacht Club gang."

Andy and the parrot were now working together to stop Olga from dropping José overboard. The parrot Maxi flew up close to Olga's face, squawking and flapping. She dropped the dog.

Andy was trying to work around the flapping parrot and managed to catch José. The parrot landed on José's head, then looked up at Olga. He was silent as though he was thinking.

"You fucking linebacker, leave my friend José alone, or next time, you will have to deal with me. I'll take your eye out and make a pirate out of you. Like I did with the last guy."

Andy looked at Rocco, hunched his shoulder, then asked, "Did I really hear that?"

Rocco was bent over, laughing so hard he can't answer. Olga was staring at the dog and the parrot, amazed that she has been defeated by a bird.

The captain, sitting on the rail, was laughing as hard as Rocco. He started to get up but fell backward into the bay. Rocco, still on the dock, laughingly pulled him out.

José, with the parrot still on his head, went strutting down the deck as he thought he and Maxi had just won a gang fight.

When the parrot thought all was quiet, he said, "José you have to learn some social skills. Don't pee on regular people, but Olga and Pendleton are acceptable targets, okay?"

José agreed. "Maxi," he said, "why don't we form a society for animals against men."

"Great idea, José. Why don't we include all humans except the people we like."

"Maybe," answered José, "we can get some of the seagulls to join."

Maxi got all in a flutter, then screamed, "José, you traitor. No dirty seagulls. I'm the boss bird here."

"All right, maybe we can get the two mice down in the bilge to join us."

"What're their names?"

"I don't know, but I like the idea. They probably don't have names, so let's just call them Batman and Robin."

"Okay," replied Maxi. "Do you know how to talk mice?"

"No I only talk yip, yip," replied José.

"I'll fly down to invite them into the society. I hope they talk yip, yip because I don't talk mice either."

"I'm sure they do. They are from China also," answered José.

Meanwhile, Olga has fallen instantly in love with Andy. The captain wants Olga to get the crew together in the saloon to figure how they are going to pay for boat expenses between here and Key West.

******

Pendleton's sister Iris was coming from England for a two-week visit. He wanted to con her into being a partner because bed and bath in England are popular. He told Billie and Deana to entertain her, then sent Andy to pick her up at the airport in Rocco's truck.

Andy arrived at the airport to find a pretty, fiftyish woman looking lost, so he focused on her.

"Iris!" he yelled. "Is that you?"

Iris looked at Andy and smiled. She was not totally surprised that a handsome young man would know her so far away from home.

"Yes, it is," she replied. "Who are you, dear?"

"I'm Andy. Your brother sent me to pick you up. Are you all right?"

"Yes, dear, I'm fine. Where is your automobile?"

"I will be your personal servant for the day, and this is it," he answered. He bowed and waved his arm and hand, tipped with a Boston Red Sox cap, Three Musketeers–style, at a very old rundown red ice cream truck.

"What the hell is this blooming piece of junk? How come my brother didn't send a limo?"

"He is on his yacht. He doesn't have an automobile yet."

"You mean he didn't bring the MG on the back deck? I should have had my Rolls shipped over. God, this truck stinks to high heaven. Do you have a dead animal under the bonnet?"

"No, that's my friend Rocco's garbage. He throws all his left-overs in the ice cream bay."

Iris turned her nose up at the thought of the garbage in back. She glanced up at the visor and saw a to-do list. The first item was to clean out the ice cream bay in back. "How old is this list, Andy?"

"I don't know. It's been there since I meet him three months ago."

Iris looked at Andy and said, "I can only imagine what his home looks like."

"Iris, you would be surprised at how clean he is at home. It's immaculate."

"Andy, I must change the subject. My Coco is still in the receiving area at customs. Tomorrow you will have to retrieve her for me."

"That will be up to my boss."

"Believe me, you will be attending to my pussy in the morning."

"I would like to be attending to it right now," Andy mumbled.

"What did you say, dear?"

"I hope to see you later," Andy replied.

******

Pendleton waited impatiently at the top of the gangplank to greet her. The parrot was on the roof, and José was beside Pendleton, deciding whether or not to pee on Iris. The two mice were hiding to observe the new arrival.

Pendleton smiled as Iris stepped out of the truck. "Good to see you, dear sister," he called out.

Iris waved and replied, "Come down here immediately and retrieve my luggage, then give me a hug."

The captain looked at Olga standing beside him, slightly behind. "Olga, go fetch her bags and bring them to her suite."

Iris, now at the top of the gangway, was taken aback and whispered to Pendleton, "My god, who is that? She looks like the terminator."

"She is the cook, and she cooks like a terminator. If you don't get sick looking at it, you certainly will by eating it."

"Have you added any shoes to your collection, brother?" The captain gestured toward the stem.

"Come in and sit down, dear."

Billie and Olga were listening and wondering what this shoe thing was all about. Pendleton and Iris now sitting on the back deck in the shade were being served tea and crumpets by Deana.

Pendleton quickly started talking to Iris about the bed and breakfast. Iris was eating a gross-looking sandwich she had brought with her. Deana and Billie watched from across the saloon.

"Deana, what kind of crap is she eating?" asked Billie.

"I think it's a cucumber sandwich. It's the equivalent of an English Big Mac," Deana replied. "I guess it keeps her regular."

"Are they to cheap to buy cold cuts?" asked Billie.

Deana replied, "Look at them legs. Do you think you will look that good at fifty something?"

"I guess I'm going to start eating cucumber sandwiches," replied Billie.

At this time the dog, José decided to make friends with Iris, instead of peeing on her foot. He snuggled up to her well-shaped calf, then looked up.

Iris felt him and looked down, thus making eye contact.

"Look, Penny, what a cute little Pekingese. What's this little creature's name?" She then bent down to give him a cucumber out of her sandwich, but José was not interested. He looked back at the mice hiding under the chair and said, "Yip, yip, don't bother, kids. Leave it there it's awful."

The mice hunched their shoulders as if to say, "We're hungry."

Batman suddenly turned and said to Robin, "Let's go to our stash in the kitchen."

"Good idea," replied Robin. "It turns out to be a good thing that we steal it before Olga cooks it."

"You're right. Imagine eating it after it's cooked." Batman laughed.

José followed them into the kitchen. "Hey guys," he whispered, "I hear we are going to have a new arrival."

Robin asked, "What is it?"

José replied, "A cat."

Batman and Robin both screamed, "Cat!"

By now, the parrot Maxi had arrived. "Cat," he squawked, "poison the cat."

Batman said, "Don't worry, Maxi, I've dealt with some pretty mean damn cats before. Hot pepper will get her trained to see things our way pretty quick."

Maxi asked, "How is that going to train him? He will just try harder to kill us."

"Well, Maxi, it goes like this. The cat gets hungry. After a while, we break out some of our supplies and make a deal with her. She will see things our way for the food."

Robin cut in and assured Maxi. "Don't worry, Maxi. It works, believe me. We have gotten rid often cats already since we moved aboard."

"I hear someone coming," José whispered. "We are not supposed to be in the giant's kitchen, and I think it's her."

"She is a nice lady," replied Robin. "She leaves us food."

"Yeah, it's probably rat poison. Be careful," whispered Maxi. Just then, the floor started to shake.

"It's her. I'm getting the hell out of here," Maxi grumbled.

"Yeah, me too," repeated José.

"We're staying. We live here," echoed the mice.

José replied, "No, let's meet in our conference room under the couch in the saloon in ten minutes sharp. We still have to figure out how to handle the cat. I do hope I can take her."

They all agreed, then scattered.

******

"Penny," Iris whispered, "do send that cute young boy Andy to tend to my pussy."

Pendleton was amazed that another animal will be onboard and replied, "Oh goody, just what I need, another fleabag running under foot. What the bloody hell is this, Noah's ark?"

Iris stared directly at Pendleton and replied, "Is it any worse to have an award-winning pussy on board than a first-class shoe sniffer. Don't forget my Coco has more titles than you will ever have, and he has only one"

The captain ignored her comment and sat.

"Penny, I brought a surprise for you. Do you want to see it now?"

"Well, I might as well."

"It's in my bag. I'll get it. Wait here."

Iris soon returned with a gift-wrapped package. "Here open it, dear," she said as she handed it to him.

Pendleton, happy that his sister has thought of him, opened the package with great anticipation. "What is it? I can't wait."

He finally got through all the paper and held up an expensive pair of size 10 Italian heels.

Billie looked at Deana. "There is something strange about this captain."

Deana answered, "I know him well. He is all man under the sheets but can sometimes be a bit girly in public."

"Oh, now, I'm getting it. No wonder he's so uptight. He always has the rag on. You had better get him a loser girdle for his next birthday."

Iris, feeling giddy after having just one Billie punch, consisting of homemade liquor and cheap store bought fruit juice, wanted to know about Andy. She was secretly planning to have a rump with him.

"I say, my sweet brother, would you have Andy knock me up in the morning?"

"Iris, don't you think he's a little young for you?" Billie Joe called. "Use protection? I want him next."

Deana smiled. "Billie, that term just means to wake somebody up."

Pendleton was getting a kick out of the English language barrier.

"Iris,"—he laughed—"myself and the girls along with this zoo will winter in Key West."

"That's nice, Penny. Maybe I'll visit this winter to get warm."

Iris had long ago developed a habit for afternoon tea. She was currently lose enough for the captain and the girls to hit her up for a partnership.

"I like this American long island iced tea much better than the British afternoon tea. There is no tea bag, and it has a big punch."

"Iris, we need your help with this project," replied the captain. "They like bed and breakfast in this country. We have a good schedule, and I need money for advertising. Our old friend Daniel Murphy has secured a slip for us in Key West."

"Tell me more, brother. I'm looking for something to do to keep me busy."

"Iris, the bed and breakfast is yuppie or uppy something like that. We need money to print brochures. Deana will take care of that."

Iris secretly controlled Pendleton's money through his estate because the queen ordered it to be that way. She liked the idea of a bed and breakfast and was becoming quite excited about the project.

"I will advance you some money. When will we be off to Key West? That Daniel is such a man with his ten-inch king's tool for pleasure in his pants. I can't wait to join him again. Billie, would you pass me the Chenille Number 5?"

******

After a month of leisure aboard the boat in Manhattan, Iris wanted an accounting from her brother, Captain Pendleton, regarding the money spent. The captain has no written records, just a pile of receipts. While discussing expenses, he told Iris that some of the pounds spent may seem wasteful, but they are getting the boat ready to head for the Key West.

"Iris, we need lots of fuel to get there. We need food and, most of all, advertisement in Key West."

"Penny, you must keep better records. Soon or later, the American government will check on you."

"Iris, I don't know much about record-keeping. The boat needs some updating to attract the elite wealthy clients that I want on board. We will want people such as ourselves to converse with. I will not comingle with the commoners. Your elegance will help us. You and Deana can go to the local antique stores to pick up some tiffany lamps and other fancy objects. This is pertinent to our success. The yacht must overwhelm our guest with old world ambiance."

Iris, thinking that her brother was holding out on her, whispered, "I'm horny, not stupid. You were an officer in the Royal Navy. Certainly, you know how to keep records."

She stood to finish her dialogue.

"I like America. I'll stay awhile to make sure you use the rest of the money properly. On second thought, I'll spend the rest properly. Deana and I will buy very good reproductions. The guest won't be any the wiser."

The captain, somewhat surprised by his sister's business sense, stood also.

"I think business is done," he announced. "We shall head for Boodles to celebrate our new venture. I'll call the rest of our crew to celebrate with us."

******

Booties bar was a mixture of artist, writers, eclectic kooks and dreamers, gay and straight. If you're odd, transgendered, or creative and live in Manhattan, you drink at Booties.

Booties owner Nicole watched the group come in. She took time to introduce herself. Nicole kept checking Iris out, along with Billie and Deana, paying personal attention to Iris. She quickly got used to Pendleton. After introducing herself, she sat with them.

"I would like all of you to be my guest. Booties is having a drag show this evening, starring Amy Damarlo." As an afterthought, she added, "Pendleton, you are invited also."

The group, in unison, raised their drinks, then shouted, "Hear, hear."

Iris was drinking her second long island iced tea, which she compared to the drinks Billie makes.

"I like the boat drinks better."

Nicole, somewhat offended, said, "Iris, please allow me to personally make a Tahitian slinger for you. I guarantee that you will enjoy it."

"Nicole, I hope I didn't hurt your feelings. Of course, I'll take the Tahitian slinger."

When Nicole returned with the personalized drink, Iris thanked her, then said, "Nicole, we are going to Key West on the yacht."

Nicole replied, "I own a bar there also. Maybe I can ride down with you aboard the boat."

Iris returned the conversation saying, "We are going to start a bed and breakfast on Lord Pendleton's yacht."

Nicole had a surprised look on her face. "That man is a lord!" She then looked at Penny who was chatting up some men at the bar. "Hard to believe, isn't it?" She paused, took a second look at him, and said, "I am going to live in Key West also, Iris. I may be able to help with your local events to try to attract customers for the boat."

Iris, still dwelling on Nicole's remark, answered, "Nicole, be careful what you say about the captain. We share the last name."

"You're married to him!"

"Oh no, my dear," Iris said, then smiled. "He is my, sad to say, brother."

******

Andy and Rocco entered Booties, and Andy got right to work, trying to explain to Rocco about lesbians and gays. As they chatted, he ordered a fizzle drink with a funny name.

"Rocco, this is an alternative lifestyle bar. It's known as a neutral zone. There is no sex, no big shorts, no poor people, no tough guys. Everyone gets along just as they are."

"We have petunias in Boston also," replied Rocco. "What's this neutral crap, and what the hell kind of drink is that?"

"Rock, it's mixed. It's not only gays. There are tyrannies here along with writers and other creative people."

"I want a beer and a shot," Rocco yelled at the waitress.

She was busy but rushed over to quiet him down before anyone was offended.

"We don't have whisky or beer," she scolded. "You have to order from the menu. If you don't like it, you can leave."

"Rock, they only have fancy stuff here."

"Andy, let's get out of here. I can't stand these high-class snobs."

"Rock, let's finish our drink first."

"What drink? They don't have anything here that I would drink. We need to go to a man's bar, not this sissy bar."

"Rock, slow down. Look around at the ladies present. Why don't you pick one out?"

Iris heard all the noise and glanced at Rocco and Andy. She wanted an introduction so she sent the captain over to invite them to the table for drinks.

Rocco eyed Billie Joe, and Deana then agreed to sit with them.

"Isn't your friend coming over also?" Iris asked, then turned to the captain and whispered, "I want the other one, not him."

Rocco overheard her and stormed away from the table to get Andy.

"Hey, Andy!" he shouted across the room. "The old one wants you. I'll take the young blonde."

Andy smiled at Rock and headed for the table. "Andy, how old are you?" Iris asked.

"Twenty-six."

"You speak well and seem educated. You're far too handsome to be a deck hand. I have a better opportunity to offer you."

"I'm involved with a college for my doctorial."

"Andy," she replied, "Rocco is like a hyper fox terrier. Please keep him in check. Myself and the girls are departing now. You and Rocco stay out of trouble."

"Sure, but what is the better opportunity all about?"

"Come back tonight for the show, and we can talk. Please leave the terrier at home."

Episode 2

Docked in Manhattan, the yacht rested glamorously amongst the other big boats. The month of July was hot and sticky. The weather this year was unusual. Aboard the yacht, Lord Pendleton and his crew sat in the saloon, discussing, acquiring paying guest.

Coco, a Siamese cat belonging to Iris, had finally settled in on board, much to the distaste of the rest of the animal gang. She didn't like birds, dogs, nor mice. Coco doesn't like anyone, period.

Nicole, who runs Booties bar and sponsors an occasional contest, was helping. She and Deana were trying to figure out how to structure the brochure for first-class guests.

"Deana," Iris asked, "how is the ad coming for the paper?"

"Iris," Nicole answered, "Deana and I have some good ideas. We have decided this package is going to be all inclusive."

"Very well. Can we make more money that way? Do keep in mind that we are only interested in high-class people. Hold that thought, I have to give my Coco some milk to drink."

José, Batman, Robin, and Maxi were observing from their meeting place, under the couch. They observed Iris reaching into her pocketbook and removing a nip of Irish whiskey, then adding it to the cat's bowl.

The society of pets against people were in horror. "Look!" says José. "She is giving Coco booze."

"I know," replied Maxi. "That eats a lush."

Batman joined the conversation. "We don't have to train that cat. All we have to do is stay out of her way when she gets drunk and falls down."

Billie Joe, having just arrived with drinks and food, gave her two cents worth to Deana.

"The rich people I worked with on the planes didn't like to use money. I would think all inclusive would be right up their alley." She served the drinks and sandwiches, then asked, "But what about the off season, how will we pay our expenses?"

Iris, talking to the captain about expenses, answered, "Billie, why don't you figure out the social activities and include a menu for the middle class."

Billie Joe quickly figured that for the middle-class passengers, she will steal empties from Booties bar and refill them with her own beer and label it as an import. She will keep half of the money on each bottle for herself.

"Iris," she said, "for special cheap punch, I will get some supermarket brand booze and concentrated juice, then doctor it with my homemade moonshine direct from the engine room. I will get other formulas from my uncle. He was a master still man. He made the best moonshine in the county. The revenuers could never catch him."

"Billie, that's a great idea. Why don't you buy some good booze so we can refill the bottles with your moonshine. We will have that dreadful person Rocco be the taster. Maybe we can make him sick."

At that time, they all focused on Olga who was complaining about José.

Andy helped interpret again. He learned to decipher her strange language and was trying to explain to the others what she was talking about.

"Something about urine," he yelled over the noise.

Maxi the parrot has joined in with loud squawking and cursing. "Olga is a big Russian whore," he said, repeating it three times.

Olga wasn't sure what was said, but judging from the smile on José's face, she knew it wasn't good. She swung her broom at the bird but missed and hit the captain in the face, knocking him back a few steps. The captain recovered somewhat, then passed out. José started licking his face until he came to.

Maxi was squawking and laughing. "Look at Mary, what a puff!" he screamed.

The captain got to his feet and glared at Olga, then José and Maxi.

"Olga, clean up and get dinner ready," he yelled. He started to leave, then realized how bad her cooking was. He then turned and said, "Never mind, we will eat out at Booties tonight."

******

Olga, the so-called Russian cook, has returned to her cabin. José and the mice were in there also, hiding under the bed.

Robin asked, "José, are you going to let that big Russian ape get away with embarrassing you in front of everyone?"

"Hell, no," squeaked Batman. "He wants revenge. Don't you, José?"

José did indeed want revenge for her earlier outburst concerning him. "What will you do, José?" asked Batman.

"I will do what I do best, of course. Allow me to show you. If you two would be so good as to retrieve one of her shoes for me, I would appreciate it."

The two mice quickly teamed up and dragged one of her shoes under the bed.

"José, you're my hero," Robin whispered.

"Mine too," added Batman.

José smiled again. "Now for the grand moment."

"Drum roll, please?" added Batman.

José then lifted his left leg so high he almost fell over.

"Bombs away!" He giggled and proceeded to fill her shoe singing, "Pop, pop, fizz, fizz. Oh, what a relief it is."

"Boy, what a stink," squeaked Robin.

"What are you talking about?" answered José. "My pee doesn't smell."

Maxi squawked, "Sure and my shit doesn't stink either."

"It's not your pee I'm talking about, José. It's her feet," replied Batman.

Robin pushed the shoe back to where it was. "Yeah, it's pretty bad. All the East Germans had to do was throw two of her shoes near the wall, and it would have fallen over."

Billie entered Olga's room to tell her about supper and saw Olga's shoes. She smelled the urine mixed with foot odor and knew Olga was the one causing the smell aboard the ship.

José saw the open door, smiled, and left to go up on deck. Maxi followed. The mice took the shortcut through the cracks.

José entered the saloon and bumped into Iris. She loved him, even though he was a little devil. "Pookie," she whispered to him, "I want you to meet Coco so you two can be friends. Coco has always had trouble keeping friends, and I'm hoping you will be different."

José was well aware why Coco has trouble with everyone. He considered him a drunk. José looked at Iris and started to back out off the room before the cat woke from his stupor. Unfortunately, he was too late. The cat had come too and had one eye on him and the other on the dish full of whiskey in front of him. José knew the cat was too big and he won't be able to take him without the help of the others, so he started yip yipping to attract them.

Maxi was the first on the scene. "José," he yipped, "what is the matter?"

"Maxi, thank God, you're here. The cat is eyeing me. I might need help to put him down, even though he is drunk. Get ready to distract him if he moves on me, okay?"

"No sweat, pal. I'll knock on his feline ass if he pulls anything."

Just then, the mice entered the room because they heard Maxi and José talking. "Hi, guys. What's up with the drunk?" Robin squeaked.

"Looks like he is almost comatose," added Batman.

"He always looks almost comatose, Batman," replied Maxi in yip, yip.

"Uh-oh," said José, "he is starting to move. Watch out, you two."

"Don't worry, kids. I'll get him," squawked Maxi using yip, yip.

The cat was now in motion toward the mice, but he was still drunk. His first mistake was to move too quickly, thus causing him not to see the parrot coming at him. His next mistake was to try to catch two young mice.

His third problem was the leg of the table he ran into and knocked himself out cold. Iris didn't see the mice nor did she know they were conversing in yip, yip. She did see the parrot diving on Coco but thought he was playing.

She watched as José walked over to the cat to see if he was dead or alive. "He's breathing," yipped José, "but his breath stinks to high heaven."

Iris was now on her way to help her beloved cat. She picked him up and put him on the chair to sleep it off so she could continue to get the boat organized. Iris has a connection with Joan Collins and wanted to use her name to sell gold package. She has invited her to spend some time in New York on board the yacht.

Right now, Iris wanted to get the crew together for her once-a-week staff meeting. She has decided to pay Andy to chauffeur her around in her Rolls. She would be able to making sure Andy was always around so she could try to get in his pants.

At the meeting, she told everyone about her connection with Joan. They all agreed that it would be a good publicity stunt. Iris gave everyone their marching orders, then turned to Andy.

"Andy," she said in a very pleasant voice, "I want you to pick Joan up at the airport tomorrow. You have to treat her with utmost care."

Andy looked at her, surprised. "I know how to handle women. I was raised as a man. In my country, we know how to work women."

"Yes, I'm sure you do, but she is a special lady."

"It won't matter. I will make her a happy lady if the opportunity comes up."

"Andy, please go to the airport and fetch her right now, if you would."

******

Joan Collins was at the airport, waiting impatiently. Andy was surprised by her beauty.

"Hi, I'm Andres. Iris sent me to meet you. I'll be at your disposal for the rest of the day."

Joan sized Andy up, gazing slowly from top to bottom, stopping at his manly areas.

"Well, young man, I see by your pants that you are very happy to see me."

Andy, realizing that he has had a male reaction to her, replied, "Yes, ma'am, you are much more beautiful than I thought."

"Thank you, Andy. I'm going to enjoy your company, I'm sure."

They arrived back at the yacht, and Pendleton was there to open the door of the Rolls for her. Iris observed this and was upset with him for not opening her door when *she* arrived. She turned to Deana and said, "I don't know if he's horny or looking for another pair of shoes."

Billie Joe replied, "It's shoes, I'm sure. I can't blame him if he is horny. She is beautiful."

Deana snorted, "What a difference Botox can make."

Iris joined in. "Deana, you seem upset. What is the matter, dear?"

"He should be here with me, not sniffing around that old lady bitch."

"Relax a bit, dear. They are friends from a long time ago back in England."

"Oh, that's it." Deana sighed. "Well, I can understand that greeting now."

Billie butted in, "Come on, I want to meet her and help with her luggage."

The animal society had gathered under a deck chair. They were curious about her.

Maxi said, "I think I'll do a fly-over."

José told him to stay in the shade and stay cool.

Robin said, "I can't wait to get into her luggage."

Batman replied, "Shall we eat a hole in the side, or wait till she opens it?"

José interceded between the mice. "Let's calm down and wait until she is aboard, then decide what to do."

By now, Joan and her vast amount of luggage had arrived in her suite, along with Andy. She quickly enticed Andy into her bed by disrobing in front of him. Andy couldn't believe his luck and just stood there, gawking at her.

"Well," she said, "are you going to join me?"

"Me? Are you talking to me?"

Maxi, who has followed her into the room, using his best human-sounding voice, said, "Hey, scoundrel, what do you need, the tooth fairy? Of course it's you, stupid."

"Did you say something?" asked Andy.

"No, I thought it was you, dear," Joan answered.

"Well," replied Andy, "I don't know what to say. I have never done it with a movie star."

"Don't worry, honey. It's done the same way as a regular girl would do it."

"Well, if you insist, I'm ready."

"Good, then pour us some wine and hop in," encouraged Joan as she pulled the sheets back.

Andy, taken aback by her beauty, stopped to enjoy the magnificent view.

Joan said, "What are you waiting for? Hurry, hop in."

Andy, still drinking in the beauty of the scene, replied, "I'm enjoying the view. It reminds me of a beautiful sunset with a pink haze floating above."

Joan replied with a big smile, "Cut the bullshit and bring that dinosaur bone over here. I can't wait to get my clock cleaned, my bells rung, and my joints rattled."

Meanwhile, the rest of the animal society has slipped into the room, unannounced. They were observing from under the dresser. Maxi was very familiar with human interrelations, but the other three don't have a clue.

"Maxi, why are they in bed going up and down?" asked Robin.

"I think they are tickling each other," said Batman.

Maxi, the knowledgeable one, said, "They are screwing, you dumb bastards."

"What's a screwing?" asked José.

"I think it's when you build something and don't get paid for it," answered Batman.

"It looks kind of hard to do," said Robin.

"Look, kids, it the way humans make babies," replied Maxi.

"Isn't she too old to have a baby? Why is it taking so long?" asked Batman.

"They are sleeping," added José, as he compared his equipment to Andy's.

Maxi saw him and said, "You're about eight inches shih, and you've been fixed. That's like tits on a bull. You better depend on your sweetness to make it with her. If you're that horny, why don't you go up on deck and rub against Pendleton's leg."

"The hell with it. Let's check out her stuff in the open luggage container," cried Robin.

The four of them instantly started stealing her stuff. José took a bra. The mice stole two pair of her silk undies.

"What are you going to do with them?" asked José.

"We will chew around the edges and make silk sheets for our bed."

The parrot grabbed a small compact and pulled the mirror out. Robin saw him and asked, "Why do you want a mirror? You're the ugliest one here."

"I'm not ugly. I'm a true-blooded Macaw, and I'm considered handsome by the humans and not to mention my mommy thinks I'm pretty also."

At this time, Andy and Joan are making so much noise, moaning and screaming that the mice suggest that they all run for cover.

"I think they are going to throw up," cried Batman. "Let's get the hell out of here."

Maxi said, "No, that's the climax. Now is when they roll over and smoke while the man promises her everything she ever wanted. The more mature women know better and usually kick the guy out of bed and tell him to leave."

José said, "Wait a minute, look, they are starting all over again."

Batman said, "I can't watch this movie again. I'm too tired. Let's get our stuff and leave."

"That's not going to be so easy," replied Maxi. "The door is closed."

"Don't worry, we can get out through our secret hole," answered Robin.

Maxi and José looked at each other, knowing they won't fit through.

"What's the matter, guys?" asked Batman. "Don't worry, we will widen it for you."

Episode 3

Iris was upset because they all went to Booties bar without her. Joan has invited Deana to her studio to get their hair done together. She had Andy pick them up in the Rolls, hoping to get him in bed again.

Deana met Joan's sister at the studio and was excited to be in their company.

"Hi, Jackie, how are you today?" she asked. "Your hair looks so soft. How do you do it?"

"Deana, what a pretty name. You're a friend of Joan's, so nice to meet you. I'm having a party at the Pear Restaurant tonight, and I would like to invite you."

The three ladies gossiped for a while. Joan decided to bring up the Eight-Inch Club, a contest between her and Jackie.

"Jackie, dear, how are you making out regarding our quest?"

"Funny you should bring that up. I noticed your driver is quite handsome."

"Yes, isn't he?"

"Have you added him to the count yet?"

"Of course I have, dear sister."

"Well, aren't you going to share him?"

"Not right now. Deana and I have to get going back to the boat before Iris blows a circuit."

Deana, intrigued by their conversation, asked, "What is the quest?"

Joan was proud to answer because she was ahead by one man.

"The quest is a contest between myself and Jackie. We are having a contest to see who can reach five hundred first."

"Five hundred what?" ask Deana.

"Five hundred men," replied Joan.

"I believe you are ahead by one driver, sis," joked Jackie

"That will take you girls forever," interjected Deana.

"Not really. We are up to 495 for me and 400 for Jackie."

Deana was awestruck and wanted to hear more, but the sisters clammed up and ended it.

"Well, good luck, girls," answered Deana. "We really have to get back to the boat now, Joan."

******

Back at the boat, Deana tells everyone she has been invited to a big shot party.

The rest of the crew were jealous and immediately started planning how they will attend also. "The hell with it!" yelled Rocco. "We will just invite ourselves and go in the door the same time as Deana."

"Good idea, Rock. We can get dressed right now and be ready," whispered Billie Joe.

"I have to supply the transportation? I can't believe they invited Deana and not me," Iris angrily replied.Olga wanted to go also. "Let's just to go," she muttered. "I don't need not to dress special."

"I'm all set," said Andy. "I'm the driver."

******

About nine o clock, the animal society watched them drive away in the Rolls. Maxi and the gang retired to the meeting room on top of the couch.

"Ah, this is fun, isn't it?" said José.

"We have the whole boat to ourselves," replied Maxi.

"Maybe we can watch a movie and eat popcorn?" squeaked Batman.

José liked the idea and headed for the microwave.

"Where are you going?" asked Maxi. "We eat it raw. It's better for your stomach."

"Not mine," replied José. "I need butter on mine."

Batman piped up and squeaked, "Make mine with cheese."

Robin added, "Me too."

"I just heard a loud noise at the companion way ladder," squawked Maxi.

"What's that?" asked Robin.

"Don't know, let's see," replied Batman as they scurried over to the door.

"Oh my god, Maxi, it's your father, the pirate," squeaked Batman.

"No, not him. I won't live with that man again. I won't leave you guys. We have to make him go away."

"Don't worry, Max," replied José. "We can get rid of him before the people come back. He's shit-faced as usual. He should be easy prey for the likes of us."

"All right," replied Maxi. "The first thing we have to do is immobilize him."

"How will we do that? He's too big for us," said Batman.

The pirate by now is rattling the door and hollering.

"Ahoy in there, you land lubbers. I'll be wanting my bird back now, or you will paying what he is worth." He paused then added, "That being five thousand dollars."

"Maxi, are you really worth that much?" asked José.

"Of course not. The man is a drunken bum."

"What are we going to do if the people come back, and he is still here. They will give you back to him," Robin said excitedly.

Coco had finally awoken after a day of drinking. She has a hangover and was very upset about the noise the pirate was making.

"I'll claw his goddamn eyes out and chew his nose off," she hissed.

"Hey, look, guys, it's the drunken cat. She looks upset."

"Yeah, I wonder what she wants."

"Let's ask her to help us. She looks like she can be pretty tough."

Maxi has been deep in thought and finally comes up with an idea.

"I got it, kids. We will drag him over to the electric boat, lift on the rear deck, and pull him up in the air."

"Great idea, Maxi, but how will we get him down to our level?" asked José.

"Easy," replied the cat in a bit of a slurred voice. "All we have to do is trip him with some rope. Then we tie the rope around his good leg and pull him over with the winch."

"Okay," said Maxi, "I'll lure him over close enough to the boat lift, then you guys knock him down."

"How are we going to knock him down? I'm too small," squeaked Batman.

"Allow me," replied Coco as she darted out the open back window.

Maxi flew up to observe the cat, then returned to his friends.

"I don't know what he is going to do, kids, but let's get the lift ready."

The pirate was now balancing on his peg leg, which has been glued together again. His bottle of whiskey was pretty much empty. He was still cursing about the stolen bird.

The people on the next yacht told him to shut up and quiet down, or they will call the police.

"Aye, ya murderous pigs," he mumbled back to them. "I'll cut your hearts out and feed you to the sharks."

The pirate swore at them again, then threw his bottle, and he missed everyone. Coco, now in position, jumped on the pirate's head meowing loudly and clawing his neck. The pirate turned suddenly, breaking his wooden leg again in the same place on the same crack as the first time.

José yelled "Attack!" and dragged the hook over from the winch. The pirate is so drunk he doesn't know which way is up.

"Don't worry, Coco," yelled Maxi. "Here, we come to help you."

"Don't give up, Coco. We have a plan," squeaked Batman and Robin simultaneously.

"I'll scratch his blooming nose off if he tries to get away," replied the cat.

"No, don't hurt him," squawked Maxi. "I like him . . . sort off."

"Are you kidding or what?" replied the cat.

"I have the hook around his leg," hollered José. "Somebody go sit on the switch!"

"I'll get it," cried the cat as he flew over the deck to the electric winch.

"Hurry!" squeaked Batman. "He's getting up."

"By Jove, ya blasted fur burgers. You be tangling with a killer, you be."

Coco has finally started reeling in the biggest fish of her life in the form of a one-legged pirate.

"Ah, ya filthy flea bags, let me loose," cried the pirate.

"Faster," squeaked Batman. "Faster, he will get away."

"Not if I can help it," hissed Coco. "He's almost up."

"This is fun," yipped José. "I wonder where the ferret is."

"Let me go ya filthy land critters," the pirate cursed again.

"You're not going anywhere but up, you drunk," replied Maxi.

Coco was still on the switch with a big smile on her face. She had spotted his reserve bottle of whiskey on the deck.

"Nobody move," she yelled. "That belongs to me."

Coco jumped toward the bottle just as the pirate was balancing on his head with his feet pointing up toward the sky.

"Coco, get back to your position, you fool," yelled Batman.

"Like hell, I've been waiting for a break to get my own stash. Iris never gives me enough."

At this point, the pirate was not sure what had hit him. Except some animals had overpowered him.

"Maxi, call the police. Tell them he is trying to break in," squeaked Robin.

"Good thinking, Robin. I will, right now."

******

The police arrived shortly after to find the pirate hung upside down and cursing to himself.

The gang had regrouped under a life boat to observe the arrest. "Excuse me, sir, is this your boat?" ask the first cop.

"No, you blithering idiot," replied the pirate. "I've been captured by a bunch of animals."

"How many were they?" asked the other cop.

"There might be four of them flea bags. One was my friend."

"Let me get this straight. Four guys jumped you, dragged you onto this boat, and tied you to this lift. One was a friend of yours. Is that correct, sir?"

"Damn right you are, me bucko. One was my parrot, Maxi, and the others were a bunch of animals he is in cahoots with."

The other cop started laughing as he handcuffed him. "We have to drop this one off at Bellevue," he said.

"What the blooming hell are you two doing to me?" yelled the pirate.

He started wiggling around as the cop was lowering him to the deck. His peg leg came undone, and he fell the rest of the way. The cops dragged him off without it. The rest of the gang just started laughing.

"I think we taught him a lesson," cried Maxi. He dialed the captain's cell phone using his beak. "Okay, now for plan B," he squawked. "I will place a call to the cab co. We will be on our way to the party soon . . . Hello, would you send a cab to the marina to pick up my pets? A dog, cat, parrot, and two mice. They will be at the curb in front of the gate. Please drop them off at the servant's entrance to the Pear Restaurant . . . Fifteen minutes is good. Come on, kids, we have to get up to the front gate."

"Wait until I hide my bottle," hissed Coco.

"Forget the bottle. It will still be here when we get back tonight," replied José.

"Yes," said Maxi, "we have to get you looking straight. Come with us to the party. They will have plenty of booze there."

"I will come to the party, but I need a stiff one first," answered Coco.

"All right, go get cleaned up. We will make you a drink," Batman and Robin offered.

"Do something about your breath," Robin demanded.

"I don't have to go anywhere to get clean. I simply wash my face with my paw," answered Coco.

******

As they watch the turban-covered head of the cab driver, the mice realized something bad was up.

"Maxi, be careful. The driver keeps looking at you in the mirror. He might know you are worth a lot of money," announced Batman.

"I know I saw his eyes," answered Maxi.

"Don't worry, gang," replied Coco. "I'll rip him a new nose if he tries anything."

"Let's get out now," said José

"No, we will be lost in the streets of New York, never to be found again," replied Batman. "

All right, knock it off, I smell something awful. José, did you poop in the cab?" asked Coco.

"No, I think it's your breath blowing back in our faces," answered José.

"It's coming from up front," added Batman.

At this point, they reached the restaurant. The driver looked over the seat and smiled, showing some missing teeth amongst the yellow remainders.

"Don't move," he said in broken English. "I will look for my pay first."

The driver, looking for his pay, left them in the cab while he searched for his money.

"God, it's him that stinks so much," said Maxi. "No wonder their flying carpets work. All that foul smell must make them rise. Let's get out of here."

"Sure, but how," replied Robin.

"It's simple," answered José as he pushed down on the window button.

"Wow, you're very smart," squeaked the two mice in unison.

The troop all jumped to the ground and entered the door of the kitchen, which was open to let out some heat. The cab driver was yelling at the chef, trying to get him to pay for the cab. The chef was holding a meat cleaver. He told the cabby to leave just, then the animal society showed up.

"They are the ones I drove here," yelled the driver as he ran toward them.

"We don't allow animals in here, and we don't want no stinking cab drivers here either," replied the chef in a very loud but controlled voice. He lifted his meat cleaver and ordered the driver out. He then turned to the animal society to order them out, but they were gone.

The animals were under the table, watching the party.

"Look there's Joan," said José. "Watch this." He sauntered over with his tail fluffing in the breeze like the plum on a palace guard.

"Oh look," Joan whispered. "It's José. How did you get here, my sweet one?"

"Look," squawked Maxi. "There's Iris."

At that instant, Coco strutted out with his head higher than his blood count.

"How did you get here, my pet?" Iris asked.

The parrot and the mice were alone. The mice figured they will not be welcome in the kitchen. The parrot flew in to see the chef.

"There you are. I must evict you," grunted the chef.

"*Je parler fran*çais," Maxi squawked in perfect French.

"Wee, you speak my language," the chef replied to Maxi. "What is your name?"

"Maxi and I want a goddamn cookie."

"Wee I have a cookie for you."

"*Merci beaucoup*," squawked Maxi, then flew out to join the mice under the table.

The party was just about over when Iris collected Coco and José not knowing that the mice and the parrot are in the room also.

"Maxi, how will we get home we must get into the Rolls?" squeaked Batman.

"You're right. Get on my back as the door opens. I'll fly you in," answered Maxi.

The ride home was uneventful Or they pulled the cab scene again and got the same driver who tried to kill them leading to a great calamity.

******

Rocco was aware of Andy's conquest of Joan and wanted to get close to her and gave it a try. He had Andy sneak him aboard under pretense to do some painting. Rocco saw a person that he thought was Joan and talked her into going to bed. They arrived back on deck one hour later where he bragged to Andy that he went to bed with Joan.

"Andy, you were right. She is fantastic in bed." Rocco smiled.

"Rock, you couldn't have had Joan. She was with me."

As they conversed about their stud powers, a pretty girl walked by and smiled at Rocco. "That's Joan. She's the one I just went to bed with," he whispered.

"Rocco, I don't know how to tell you this, but that's a man. He's a stand-in and stunt double for her."

"No, I was in bed with Joan," Rocco replied. He was adamant in his belief.

"Rock, so was I, and believe me, that isn't her. That girl used to be a man!" He giggled. "Believe me, pal."

Rock was now turning red with rage and started to follow her. "I'll kill her . . . him. That son of a bitch took advantage of me."

Andy grabbed him and laughed. "I think it's the other way around, my friend."

Meanwhile on the upper deck, the captain, busy stealing one of Joan's shoes, got caught by her.

"Captain," Joan said, "all you had to do was ask."

"Well," he replied, "maybe I can see your toe cleavage also?"

"Captain, you have some odd needs. All you have to do is look down. I have my best toe cleavage shoes on. See?"

"Oh yes, what a sight. Thank you," he said.

"Hey, there's Andy!" Joan excitedly exclaimed. "I need to speak with him. Excuse me, Captain. Andy dear, would you drive myself and Iris to Bloomingdales?"

"Sure. When?"

"Pick us up out front with the Rolls in about an hour," she replied.

They headed for Bloomingdales. Joan, accompanied by Iris, was going shopping. The Rolls has all the best supplies. Iris and Joan had champagne while the latest fashions were being modeled for them.

"Iris, you know I can supply you with more important guest if Andy will be available for my service," Joan offered with a smile.

"Well," Iris answered, "I have my sights set on him for myself, dear. I think you will have to work much harder than that to steal him away. Joan, I think I could share Andy with you under the right conditions."

"Well, dear, just what are these conditions?"

Iris, now on her third glass of champagne, replied, "I'm thinking that each time you line up someone important to stay aboard, you will get one point. Each point will be good for one hour with Andy."

"Deal," replied Joan. "I owe you one guest."

"What do you mean?" asked Iris.

"Just what I said, dear."

"You mean you already got him? You lucky tramp, you. How did you do it?"

"It just happened."

"What was it like?"

"Oh dear, he is good. You should see his thing."

"I will, I'm sure."

The ladies finished their shopping. The salesgirl at Bloomingdales told Iris and Joan they will get an extra 15 percent off for senior citizen discount. Iris gave her a look, then pepper-sprayed her. Joan reprimanded her.

"I'm sorry, sweetie. I thought it was perfume."

She went to the next counter to check out. As they headed home, they sat behind Andy, conjuring up visions of happy satisfaction. Both of them smiled.

******

Back aboard the yacht, the next morning, Iris and Nicole met with the staff. Iris liked Nicole. She was becoming close and getting tempted to make it with her because of the attention Nicole gave her. It's been a long time since she made it with a girl in boarding school.

Iris was the real leader on this boat. Deana and she were becoming good friends. Iris was getting serious about being a big shot and was dressing the part.

The crew didn't know it, but they are about to get lucky. Olga had gotten drunk again, and Rocco had stepped in to cover for her. He put a great evening meal together for cheap. The rest of the crew couldn't believe their good fortune.

"Did you know that Rocco can cook and repair things? He has been a captain on a fishing boat. He has staying power in bed to top it off," Billie Joe whispered to Iris. She smiled at the last quote.

"That's great," Iris replied. "I will pay him to be the cook. Olga can be our deck hand and helper."

"Thank God," interjected Pendleton. "I've lost ten pounds since she started cooking."

"Me too," replied Deana. "Maybe we should keep Olga. We can advertise the boat as a health spar."

"No way," Billie Joe said. "I can't afford to eat out anymore."

"Then it's settled. Rocco is the new cook," Iris said. "Billie, you two seem to have a certain relationship. Why don't you see how much we have to pay him?"

Iris kept thinking how Rocco would be in bed. She knew he's good guy, but the captain didn't like Rock.

******

The whole crew was mad at Rock because he was causing them to depart for Key West later than expected. He cannot make up his mind about being the cook and moving to the Key West.

The captain was desperate to keep his appointment in Key West to acquire the best slip from his friend, Daniel Murphy. Pendleton was desperate, so he interviewed Rocco.

"We have to leave soon, Rocco. If you won't be the cook, you can be our engineer and back-up captain."

"Look, Captain, you don't like me. How can I work for you?" replied Rock.

"I really need a cook. I'll assign Iris as your boss, and I won't be your boss."

"Okay. It's a deal, but you have to guarantee that you will not interfere. I want it in writing."

The captain was happy to have a good cook but still didn't like Rocco. "That's fine with me. Let's go. I'll drive the first four hours, and you take over the next four, then we will stop for the night."

Rocco was now the ship's chef, engineer, and second helmsman. He was a better cook than Olga, so she became the maintenance man.

Olga, in an attempt to be stronger to be able to do her new job, sneaked into Rocco's room to lift his weights. José came in to pee on her shoes while she had weights in the air. She couldn't move quick enough to stop him.

José had done his deed, and Olga was close on his tail.

"I'll boil you in oil, you little bitch."

"Help!" yelled José. "I'm coming," replied the parrot. Maxi flew in front of Olga and flapped his wings. Olga was thrown of stride and trampled Rocco's tomato garden on the rear deck as she chased José. The mice saw a couple of smaller tomatoes roll away.

"Come on, Batman," said Robin. "Let's get them for supper."

"The tomatoes are too big to fit through the hole," replied Batman.

"Don't worry, we can eat some outside."

As they tried to retrieve the tomatoes, Olga came running by, still chasing José and squashed the tomatoes with her size 12s.

"Look out! Here she comes again!" screamed Maxi in an effort to protect the mice. "We have to stop her somehow."

"Don't worry," cried Coco. "I'll take care of that." She hissed and jumped between Olga's legs. Olga tripped, hitting her head on the deck, knocking her out.

"Uh-oh, Coco," said Batman. "You've killed her."

"No, she's alive," replied José as he licked her face. "She tastes like fish."

Olga started to move and came to, looking at José with a big smile on her face.

"You sweet little doggy, you saved my life. I will never try to hurt you again!" she said.

"Don't believe her," said Coco. "She is mean to the bone."

"What going on down there?" yelled Pendleton.

Rocco came to the deck to find her and helped her up as he answered the captain.

"I don't know what happened," he hollered to the captain. "Olga, come down to the galley. I'm cooking something special for Pendleton. You can deliver it for me."

Olga smiled, knowing what Rocco was up to.

"Bring all this food into the saloon and give Pendleton this plate," Rocco said as he handed her a dish of pasta. Rocco smiled and said, "Tell him I made it just for him."

******

The yacht was on the way south again. The trip was uneventful. They tied up at Norfolk, Virginia, marina. Rock, as he did at every stop, threw his traps over the stern to catch crabs for dinner.

Pendleton suddenly appeared behind him.

"Rocco," he groaned, "the boat has been running very rough. One of the engines needs an expensive part. We don't have enough money in the kitty to fix it. We will have to travel a lot slower on the other engine the rest of the way."

"Are you sure we can't fix it?" replied Rocco.

"We can fix it, but we need a part. Do you suppose that one of those old navy boats might have what we can use?"

"Even if it does, how are we going to get it?" asked Rocco.

Just then, another voice joined in. It's Olga.

"I can get it," she said. "I know my way on ships. In Russia, we used to borrow parts all the time."

"This isn't Russia," replied Rocco. "We will get thrown in jail if we get caught."

"That's not so bad. In Russia, we get shot."

******

Rocco and Olga rowed over from the marina to the navy yard in search of engine parts. They went aboard a vessel about the same size as their boat to scavenge. As luck would have it, they found exactly what they needed and removed it.

As they exited the boat, Rock and Olga looked up to see an armed sailor peering down at them.

"Halt!" yelled the navy shore patrol guard.

"Hi," Olga replied in an effort to look innocent.

"What are you two doing on this boat?" he asked. "This is government property."

"We thought this boat was junk. We just wanted to take some pictures," replied Rocco. "I'm a marine. I have the right to be on this boat." Rocco was adamant about his rights.

"What do you have in your hand?

"I don't know. It was in my way, so I moved it."

"Where is your camera?" asked the guard. He was not as dumb as Rock had hoped for. "You're a jarhead thief!" called out the navy man. "The navy considers you marines aboard ship as sea-going bellboys."

Rock didn't like his attitude at all and was about to attack when the navy guy aimed his pistol in the general direction of him and

Olga. "The two of you come out of there now," commanded the navy man.

"All right," replied Olga as she reached up for his hand to steady herself.

The guard, in an effort to be a gentleman, extended his hand, not realizing how big Olga was.

She pulled on him to leave the boat. Instead of her moving, he went into the water. She dove in.

"I will help," she yelled as she hit the water.

"Hurry, I can't swim!" he called out.

"What kind of navy guy can't swim," replied Rocco. "That's impossible. You guys are always diving for the soap in the shower."

The patrol guard was underwater and didn't hear Rocco. Olga had him by the hair and was swimming toward the dock. Rocco ran down the dock to help pull him out. The two of them pulled on him until they got him on the dock.

"Olga, give him mouth to mouth," yelled Rocco.

The guard came to as Olga was kissing him instead of giving mouth to mouth. Rocco was still busy doing chest compressions.

The guard was happy to be saved by Olga. He wanted to show his appreciation.

"Wait here until I get changed into some dry clothing," he said with a smile. "Then I'll come back to arrest you."

The two of them understood his meaning and scurried back to the yacht with their prized part in hand.

******

Rocco and Olga were trying to finish installing the stolen part. The captain, in uniform, was overseeing everything. He was being a pain in the ass as usual. "What's taking so long, Rocco?" Pendleton asked.

"Leave me alone," replied Rocco. "I'm almost done. Olga, hand me that wrench," he said to her in an effort to break off chatting with the captain.

"What's going on, Pendleton?" Maxi asked.

"Nothing, you stupid bird. Get lost before I pluck your ass clean."

Maxi just couldn't stand the captain's arrogance, so using a voice that sounds like the captain, he asked, "What's taking so long, Rocco, you stupid ass."

Rocco, thinking it's the captain, stood up and hit his head. The parrot, still sounding like the captain, started laughing. The captain looked at the parrot and started to reach for him. Olga stood also and accidentally dropped the heavy wrench on the captain's foot.

Rocco, meanwhile, was rubbing his head. Maxi flew out of the captain's way and, again using Pendleton's voice, said, "Olga, you dumb Russian slut, you hurt my foot."

Olga picked up the wrench and chased the captain around the engine room until he exited. He came back to the engine room to find it empty.

In an effort to ensure that the boat would not have any other problems, he removed his white jacket and slacked down to his satin bikinis and slid in behind the starboard engine. He intended to change the oil and air filters on both engines but was pleasantly surprised to see that Olga and Rocco had already taken care of the maintenance.

The parrot was still sitting on the engine. "Look how white you are, girly man," he squawked. "What a sissy."

The captain threw the filter in his hand at the parrot and broke one of the fuel lines.

The parrot laughed at him, then started singing a childhood limerick, "Pendleton is no friend of mine. He steals girls undies all the time. He wears them inside out just to keep the germs off his little snout. He also steals their heels to walk about. He's a pervert there is no doubt." Maxi then flew out of the room.

Olga came back to put her tools away and caught the captain in his stolen silk undies. "American men all sissies," she grunted.

Rocco came back because the parrot Maxi told him the captain needed help. "Olga, don't tell me you're that hard up," he said and started to laugh.

"No, don't you worry, Rock. Never could I be that horny."

The captain was quickly getting dressed. Olga smelled the diesel fuel. "Captain," she asked, "what happened?"

"Rocco," he said, "you and Olga have to repair that fuel line."

"Sorry, pal, you broke it, you fix it," replied Olga.

"You two are the crew. I am the captain!" he cried.

"Olga will work with you. I'm not getting near a guy with girl's undies on," replied Rocco. "I have to get clean."

"Come on, I'll help you with it," he said.

"Yes, Captain, you broke it, you fix it," replied Olga.

Rocco went back to his cabin to take a shower and used up all the hot water. The captain finished his work and went to wash his hands. The hot water was gone. He knew Rocco had to be the culprit. He always used all the hot water every time he showered.

"There are other needs for this hot water, you know," he said, glaring at Rocco.

"Listen, shithead," Rocco hollered at him. "You just got free parts and a free installation. I almost got arrested, and you're worried about some hot water."

The captain was obstinate as usual. "That has nothing to do with your inconsideration," replied the captain. He then swirled around and left, slamming the door behind. Rocco was totally disgusted with Pendleton and decided to doctor up his next meal.

******

Now that the engines were running properly, Rocco, Billie Joe, Olga, and Deana decided to visit the marina bar. Within five minutes, Rock started a fight with one of the locals. A loud debate concerning the Red Sox and the New York Yankees broke out. The local says the Yankees were better. Rock did not agree.

"The Yankees suck," yelled Rock. He swung at the man's face. "Steinbrenner sucks too," he added as his fist landed on the guy's chin.

The local guy's two friends stood to help him against Rock. Olga and Billie Joe stood for Rocco.

"Look, boys, he has girls to fight for him," the other man said.

"Olga," Rock hollered, "take care of my light stuff." He then pointed toward the local's helpers.

"You two shitheads sure you want to deal with me?" cried Olga.

One of the rebels swung a chair. "She's built like a caddy complete with bumpers," he yelled as the chair hit Rocco in the face. Olga punched the guy and knocked him out cold. The other fool jumped on her back.

"I'll get him!" Billie Joe yelled.Billie Joe pulled on him, and suddenly, his pants and undies came down, exposing his butt. Olga pulled him off by his hair, then body-slammed him on the bar. He got up, tried to walk out, and immediately took a header landing smack on the middle of his face.

"Where do you think you're going? I'm not through with you." She grunted, then sat on him.

"Do you give up?" she asked.

"Yes, I quit!" he replied.

"Good idea," she answered, then threw him on top of the other one.

"Deana," cried Billie Joe sarcastically. "Thanks for all the help."

"I helped," replied Deana. "I wished you would win. I have one of my best blouses on."

Episode 4

They were close to their Key West marina slip. The boat was in dire need of diesel fuel and supplies. They had to anchor instead of tying up. Iris had not transferred enough funds to cover the trip south. They are all gathered at the rear saloon discussing the situation.

"I know what to do!" exclaimed Rocco. "Olga, follow me."

"What are we doing?" she asked.

"To the engine room. We will need a hose about one half inch in diameter. We are going to take the fuel out of the generator tank and pump it into the main tank to run the engine the rest of the way."

Iris wasn't sure this is a good idea.

"Rocco, if you do that, won't you make a smelly mess?"

"No, Iris," answered the captain. "They can use the electric pump to transfer the fuel."

"Let's go," Olga said. Rocco Olga and the captain headed for the engine room to find the needed hose and pump.

They took about one hour to complete the process. The fuel was transferred, but to their surprise, they can't run the electric generator to refrigerate and air condition the boat.

"Captain, why didn't you think of this?" asked Iris.

"I did," he replied. "We either stay here and be cool, or we move and get into our slip at the marina tonight. Take your choice."

Iris paused, then replied to Pendleton's scenario. "I'll call Daniel Murphy for help"

"I'll pray to God," replies Deana.

"I'm having a drink," Billie Joe added.

The animal society was meeting under the couch. They really didn't care about the situation.

"Maxi," said Batman, "what should we do about food?"

"Don't worry, kid. The humans won't go hungry. We will always get their crumbs"

"I'm not waiting for the crumbs," replied Robin.

"Me neither," added Batman. "Let's hit the kitchen before everything rots."

Olga and Rock were cleaning up from the fuel exchange and having a drink from Billie's moonshine still, which was gurgling away in the engine room.

"Boy, this is weak," Olga said. "Russian vodka is better than this. We drink a gallon a day at home."

Rocco gave her a look. "Olga, you must have a stomach made of cast-iron," he said.

They were north of Key west. The boat was underway again for hours after the fuel exchange. They had just passed Stock Island and were now headed to the marina. The fuel transfer was almost gone. Pendleton had shut down one engine to conserve fuel.

Murphy had been in contact by radio and had decided where to catch up with them. He met them traveling on the gulf side near the end of the Stock Island. He arrived with ten big plastic jugs of fuel. Murphy always had the hots for Iris. He didn't know she was aboard until she called him.

"Iris, so good to see you!" he said.

Iris was becoming anxious to see Nicole, but she knows what Murphy has to offer.

"Daniel dear, so good to see you." She looked at his lower body.

"I have missed your . . . I mean, you so."

"Well, Iris," he replied, "maybe we can get together after you folks settle down in your marina slip."

"Not so fast, Daniel," she answered. "We have a lot of talking to make up for lost time."

"Iris, tell me about this Rocco guy."

Murphy appreciated Rocco's thinking: using the fuel from the generator to run the boat. He liked Rocco and knew he was a good cook. He wanted to steal him. "Rock is a jack of all trades," she replied.

"Well, he seems like a good man to have aboard a boat or restaurant."

"Yes, you're right. He is an expert Italian cook," replied Iris.

"Maybe you can introduce us?" asked Murphy.

"Certainly as soon as him and Olga finish pouring the fuel into the tanks, dear."

******

Rocco just met Murphy and was holding back. He did not make friends quickly.

"Rock, I understand you're a jack of all trades."

"Who told you that?" he growled.

Billie Joe joined in. "Iris did, Rock. I hope you don't mind, but we think you are someone special."

"I did," said Iris.

"Oh look! There is the marina. It's beautiful!" Billie Joe cried out.

The boat arrived at the slip in Key West.

Murphy takes the opportunity to hire Rocco.

"Rocco, here is my card. I could use a good man like you. Call me. I will pay you well for your services."

The slip was not as good as they thought it would be.

"I feel it is run down and below standards for our very special guest," Pendleton quoted.

"Pendleton," replied Murphy, "things are limited down here. You will have to take what you can get."

Iris called a quick meeting.

"I need to get off this boat," she said. "I want to go to see Nicole and have a stiff boat drink at the bar."

Sitting at the bar talking to Deana and Billie Joe, Rocco said, "Iris needs to get laid." "The boat needs to be painted," interjected Pendleton.

Rocco had no idea of doing it. "Don't look at me!" he yelled. Pendleton ordered Olga to do it.

Olga, Rocco, Pendleton, and Billie Joe were seated in the rear saloon, having a discussion on the color needed for the boat.

Rocco said, "All I have is a collection of old paint cans."

"Well," replied the captain, "we will have to get some money from Iris."

Rocco replied, "I'm going out for a beer."

"I will also," added Olga.

They both headed to the local redneck bar. Rock liked the prices but not the rednecks. Olga liked both. Four hours later, they decided to head home to the boat. On the way back, they passed a house under construction, ready for painting.

"Look, Rock, lots of paint," she said as she pointed toward a palette of house paint.

"We can use that to paint the boat, Olga," replied Rocco.

Rock and Olga thought for a second. Olga grabbed two buckets of paint, and Rocco followed her. Resembling two little kids, they ran like hell.

"Iris, we have good paint and need some money to pay for it," Rocco said.

Iris gave him a check to pay for the paint.

"Iris, I can't use this. I need money. The guy told me to pay cash."

"Rock, I can't give you cash. I won't be able to keep proper records."

"Well, I will have to bring the paint back to him."

"Rocco, I have to talk to the captain, then I will let you know."

"Well, don't take too long. The guy won't wait."

Rocco turned to Olga. "Come on, let's go drinking. When we get paid for the paint, I'll show you how to apply it," he told her.

On the way off the boat, they met up with Deana and Billie Joe.

"Hi, girls," Rock said with a smile.

"Hi, Rocco," Billie answered.

"Where are you two off to this fine day?" replied Deana.

Olga answered, "We get drunk, then paint boat yeah."

Deana glanced at the Rock, then smiled. "What are you going to use to paint with? Did you know we have spray equipment in the engine room?"

"I'll worry about that when I get to it," answered Rocco. "Rocco and I go drinking on the redneck bar. Okay, you two join us," Olga says in her hard-to-understand Russian accent.

"Rocco, this truck smells awful," Billie Joe said.

"Olga, your lap is as hard as a rock," Deana cried out.

"You two stop complaining," ordered Rocco. "It's the only thing we have. I just bought it. It used to be a hearse. You know, the car they throw all the flowers in on the way to the grave. It only has a bench seat, but we all made it. Didn't we?"

The bar they were going to was half-owned by Daniel Murphy. Just as they arrived, they met Daniel. He bought some drinks, so he can sweet-talk Rocco and steal him away.

"So, Rocco, have you considered my offer yet?" Daniel yelled over the noise.

Deana was wise to him. "Daniel," she said, "Rocco has a long-term commitment to the yacht. I don't think he will be joining you anytime soon."

"Rock, is Deana speaking for you?" Daniel asked.

"I'm not sure what I will do," Rocco answered.

"Well, the offer is there any time you want to join my team."

"I'll let you know," Rocco answered.

Olga suddenly jumped up and glared at Daniel. "You touch leg," she said.

"It's all right, Olga. I wanted to see if you had hair on them. I like hairy legs."

Olga was upset. "Rocco is only one who touch me," she hollered, then bent down and picked him up by his shirt. Daniel wasn't sure what had happened when he awoke a moment later, but everyone else had witnessed the punch he took from Olga.

He looked all around. In an effort to wake himself up, he shook his head. "Give me a drink!" he yelled. "What happened to me?"

By now, his bouncer was at the scene, eyeing Olga. Daniel told him to back off before she knocked him out also.

"Good god, Olga! What a punch. How would you like a job working for me as a nighttime bouncer?"

Rocco was standing between the bouncer and Olga and answered for her, "Hey, Daniel, neither one of us is available for hire.

Let it go. If you need a cook that bad, we will work sometimes, when you are shorthanded."

"That's a deal, kids," he answered as he got to his feet to regain his composure. "Bartender, another round of drinks for my friends," he yelled over the bar noise.

"Deana, did you see the way she hit him?" asked Billie Joe.

"Billie, did you catch the part when she said Rocco is the only one to touch her?"

"Yeah, there must have been something going on. Don't ya think?"

"Did Rocco say when he was going to paint the boat?"

"I think he's waiting for Iris to give him some money for paint," replied Billie Joe.

"I heard him and Penny arguing the other day about it. Penny told him to paint the boat, or else he, was fired. Rock said he was depending on the boat for a place to sleep."

"Sounds serious," answered Billie Joe. "I hope Rocco isn't fired. We won't have any more good food."

"No," replied Deana. "I don't think Penny is that stupid. Besides, Iris would never stand for it. Here comes Olga. Let's ask her about it."

"Hi, Olga, how are you today?" asked Billie Joe.

"I would be fine. Are you two also good?"

"Olga, we were wondering," replied Deana, "if you knew when the boat will be painted?"

"Oh yes, tomorrow, Rock and me paint fast with a rollers to cover the boat instantly," she answered.

"Good luck, Olga. I hope you do a good job on it," answered Deana.

******

Olga and Rocco finally got all the supplies together to paint the boat.

"Rocco, what do you like of this color I mix up?" asked Olga.

Rocco looked at her mustard-yellow paint and realized he can blame her for the horrible color when the captain blows a fuse.

"Olga, that is beautiful. The captain will love it."

"I hope you are right. We paint now, yes?"

"Yeah, here is the roller. Just roll it on the pan and then roll the paint on the boat like this," Rocco said as he demonstrated the technique to her.

"Olga," Rock said after all the paint was on the yacht, "how do you like it?"

"I think it is loud," she replies. "Great, just what I wanted," answered Rocco. "Let's get cleaned up and head for the redneck bar."

"Yeah," Olga replied, then jumped into the water.

"What the hell are you doing, Olga?"

"Water paint. I clean up."

The captain, Deana, and Iris have stopped at Booties for some drinks.

"I say, Deana, is today the day to turn the yacht around to weather the other side?" asked Pendleton.

"No, dear, we will do that next week."

Iris, not too sure why they would turn her around, asked, "Penny, why would you do that? It will cause us to move the boarding ramp to the other side." "We move the boat around so the sun can damage each side equally."

"Oh, I see."

"Penny, let's go home now. I'm getting hungry. I can't drink any more on and empty stomach. I would love one of Rocco's great meals right now."

"Yes, me too," replied Iris. "Yes, ladies. A good idea, I believe."

The three of them headed home in the Rolls, arriving at the marina around dusk.

"Penny, look! Someone has put a different boat in our slip," said Iris.

"What a hideous color that mustard yellow is. How can anyone stay on it without getting seasick?" asked Deana.

"Yes, quite ugly, but where is my yacht. I will have to talk to the marina people," replied the captain.

"Yes, please do. I'm hungry and tired. I was looking forward to a long island iced tea, then playing with my pussy," answered Iris.

Pendleton by now has arrived at the marina office to protest the moving of his ship without being notified.

"I say, old man, what have you done with my ship?" he yelled at the marina dockmaster.

"I don't know what you are talking about," the man replied.

"My yacht is gone. It has been moved, and another boat is in my slip. That hideous-looking yellow thing," he yelled as he pointed toward his boat.

"Oh," replied the girl standing beside the dockmaster. "You're right. That is an ugly color. Why did you have Rocco paint it that way?"

"What!" hollered Pendleton. "That can't be my yacht! It is completely ridiculous. I can't be seen on that thing."

"Why don't you have Rocco and Olga paint it back the way it was?" the girl answered.

Pendleton was beside himself with anger at Rocco.

"I'll kill him," he screamed and stormed out of the office.

The girls were still standing on the dock and saw him coming.

"Uh-oh," said Deana. "He looks upset, doesn't he?"

"I'll say," replied Iris.

"What's the matter, dear?" asked Deana as he stormed past them.

"Rocco has painted my yacht this hideous color!" the captain yelled as he stormed up the gangway. "I'll show that little Italian bastard who is in charge of this ship!"

"Penny, be careful. He is a tough little Italian bastard," Deana called out after him.

"Yes, dear, do be careful," Iris added.

"Rocco, where the hell are you?" Pendleton said. "When I get my bloody hands on you, I will kill you."

Deana and Iris followed him into the yacht. They bowed their heads, trying not to look at the hideous color. The captain had stopped at the door and was examining the paint.

"God almighty," he hollered. "They painted it with a roller!" He ran his hand over the finish.

"They have ruined my yacht!" he screamed. He was becoming more upset at each turn.

"Penny, dear," said Deana. "Please calm down. You are not a young man anymore."

"Yes, dear, calm down. I will have it fixed properly for you. We can't have our guest seeing this awful yellow," replied Iris.

Pendleton was now sitting on the deck, crying and sobbing. "He ruined my yacht, that dirty little bastard!"

"It can be fixed, honey," said Deana.

"It will never be like it used to," he replied to her.

After about an hour of sobbing, he finally got his act together again, just as Rocco and Olga returned to the boat, laughing at the color as they walk up the gangplank.

"Olga," Rock slurred, "this color is worse than I thought."

"Yeah, I make good yellow," she spat out in broken English.

The captain heard them and grabbed his gun from the draw.

"I'll kill them two!" he screamed, then ran out and crashed right into them. Olga went backward over the rail and into the water. Rocco rolled down the gangplank and was out like a light at the bottom. The captain regained his footing, then tripped over Olga's bottle of vodka. He slid halfway down the gangway railing, then fell head first into the drink, landing beside Olga.

"You!" he screamed. You and him are fired. I don't ever want to see you on my yacht again. Do you hear me?"

"I hear," she answered, then reached over and pushed him under. She would have let him drown. Rocco came to just in time to save the captain from her death grip.

"Olga, let him go. He will drown soon!" yelled Rocco.

Rocco couldn't swim. He was helpless to do anything. A body flew beside him and did a nice jackknife dive. It was Iris going to the rescue of her brother. She dragged him over to the side, and Rocco pulled him out. When he came to, he saw Rocco taking turns with Olga giving him mouth to mouth.

"You saved my life, Rocco. I owe you." He spat out with a mouthful of saltwater. "Olga helped," replied Rocco.

"Help me out, you baboons," yelled Iris. She looked like a drowned water rat. Some hair was drooped over her face. Her makeup was a mess.

They all helped Iris out of the water and onto the yacht. Deana was ready with a towel and a shot of brandy for each one. Rocco and Olga went down to pack their belongings.

"Penny, dear, you can't let them go. They saved your life," Deana said. She glanced at Iris for support. Iris smiled an acknowledgement.

They knew Iris had saved him, but they didn't want to lose the cook or Olga.

"Yes, Mr. Pendleton. You have an obligation to them," replied his sister.

Pendleton looked at her, not quite sure what to say. He was still very angry at the two of them. After a few moments, he agreed.

"Very well, they can stay, but who will repaint the boat?"

"I'll take care of that," replied Iris. "Rocco will have to forfeit his pay until we get it refinished."

The captain thought this over, then grinned. He thought this was a good way to get even with Rocco.

"Very well. You go tell them I am not calm enough for that yet."

"I'll go," offered Deana.

After Deana told them they could stay, Rocco replied, "I was prepared to fix it. I have called my friend J. W. Luke Montgomery III. He is an auto body man and can fix it easily and for cheap. Olga and I will pay him and assist in the recovery project."

Deana looked at Rock, her eyes wide-open, surprised by his initiative.

"Oh good, I will give the captain the news. I'm sure Iris will be happy also. Rocco, why did you paint it such an ugly color?"

"Olga did it. She is the one who mixed up the color," he said while looking at Olga in a way, to tell her not to say anything.

"But why did you get so mad at the captain?"

"He's jerk," replied Olga.

"He told me if I didn't paint the boat, I was fired. He didn't say what color he wanted," replied Rocco.

"Well, all is well that ends well." answered Deana.

******

Luke has arrived to help with the boat and has set Rocco and Olga up with the right tools. He was cleaning up the spray equipment from the engine room.

"Rocco!" he hollered. "Why the hell did you use a roller? You left a million marks. We have to sand all of them out before we spray."

"I hate this captain. He is the biggest jerk I have ever met."

Olga was busy checking Luke out. She smiled every time he looked at her.

"Yeah," she said. "Captain is jerk."

"Rocco," Luke whispered, "she is huge. Have you done her yet?"

Rocco grinned and said no. Luke knew him too well.

"Come on, Rock. I know you. When you get drunk, you'd screw a Boston lobster."

"Rocky," said Olga. "You have fun on me, yes."

"I knew it, you horny little shit. You did get her!" replied Luke.

In an effort to change the subject, Rocco started his electric sander and moved away. "Olga, where are you from?" asked Luke.

"I from Russia."

"Do you love Rocco?"

"Rocco just sex partner."

Luke was happy to have some dirt on Rocco. He can set him up for some fun.

"Rocco!" Luke yelled.

Rocco couldn't hear him, so Luke unplugged his sander. "Rocco," he calls again.

"Who the hell turned off my sander?"

"I did," replied Luke. "Olga says you are not only the poorest man in the world but the horniest one to."

"Luke, knock it off," replied Rocco.

"Rocky, you not like me," said Olga.

"Olga, I like you. Don't tell Luke anything else."

Luke paused to think. "Rocco and Olga. I can see the wedding now," answered Luke. "Are you going to have children?"

"Luke, don't be a jerk. She's my friend."

"Don't worry, Rock. I won't tell anyone in Winthrop about your marriage."

"Luke, you must be drunk or something. Leave me alone. I have to sand the wall."

"Okay. Rock, how is the sanding coming?"

"We're all done by the end of today. You can paint the boat and make that asshole Pendleton happy."

"Hey, Rock, have you gotten any of the girls on board yet?"

"No, I'm a gentleman."

"You're the horny man, as far as I know. All it takes is a bottle of vodka and a female and you're on the way."

The animal society had been watching all this and couldn't understand most of what Luke is talking about.

"Maxi, is Luke mad at Rocco?" asked José.

"No, I don't think so. They are not yelling enough."

"I think Olga is mad at Rocco. She is upset about him saying he won't marry her," replied José.'

"I think no one is mad," answered Robin.

Iris came down to talk with Luke about the paint job.

"John," she said, "I want you to do a very good paint job. My brother is still angry at Rocco. I will pay you whatever it takes. The money will be coming out of Rocco's pay, so don't worry about the cost.

"Iris, Rocco is a friend of mine. I can't charge him. How about you and I make a deal? I'll take two weeks of vacation this winter, all expenses paid for me and my wife. How's that sound?"

"I think that will be okaydoke. But I have to ask my brother."

"Well, I'm going to paint the boat tomorrow no matter what. Then we can figure who owes what to whom."

"Yes, that will be fine. Just get rid of this hideous color for me."

"It will be gone by the end of tomorrow," replied Luke. "Iris, how did you know my name is John?"

"I have relatives in the British secret service, and they did a background check. I know about everyone on the boat."

Luke looked surprised. He smiled, then said,

"Did you know that Rock was the captain of a lobster boat named the *Rockbottom*?"

"Of course, honey, that was public record." Iris smiled again, then said, "You would be surprised what I know about you."

"Do you know how many fights he was in?"

"Of course I know everything about everyone," Iris replied with a huge grin.

"Well, what do you know about me?"

"Never mind, John. I have to go find the captain." She started to leave, then turned. "John, we are all going to the bar Booties this evening. You are invited to join us."

Nicole welcomed them to Booties and told them to relax and enjoy. She had swing and disco music ready.

Luke saw Billie Joe sitting alone and decided to get some more dirt on Rocco. "Hi, Billie, how are you this evening?" he asked.

"Fine, thank you," she answered. "Luke, I want to thank you for making the boat pretty again. I don't know what got into Rocco. The other night, when we were together, he said he was angry at the captain. I didn't know he was that mad."

Luke picked up on the phrase together and decided to find out more about Rock's adventures into amour land.

"Hey, Billie, is Rocco doing Deana also? She's just his type."

Billie blushed, then answered. "No, I don't think so. The captain and she are a couple."

"What?" asked Luke, surprised. "Are you kidding? She is his girlfriend?"

"Yeah, I know she could do better, but there is something about him that she really likes."

Luke looked at her, then replied, "He must have a giant under his belt. Don't worry, sooner or later, Rocco will get her in bed. He always gets the one he wants."

"He won't get her if I have anything to say about it," replies Billie Joe.

She looked at Luke knowing that she just gave away her secret. Luke just smiled back at her and moved over to talk with Deana. He had to find out why Rock hadn't gotten her yet.

"Deana, how are you tonight?" asked Luke. "I here you and the captain are a couple."

"Yes, Luke, we are. What about it?"

"Oh, I was just wondering. What's this thing about Pendleton's toe cleavage, and how come Rocco hasn't fallen in love with you yet?"

"He is, but I don't think he can handle a girl like me. I'm too well equipped for a stud like him."

"I don't think any girl is too much for him, Deana."

"Believe me, Luke. He won't handle what I have. He can't even enjoy this bar because of his prejudices."

"He's not prejudiced. He just doesn't like gays," replied Luke.

Iris broke into the conversation.

"Luke, there you are. I have to ask you a favor. Can you take my Rolls back to Boston to be repainted?"

"Well," replied Luke, "I already have tickets. Who is going to pay for that, and who is going to accompany me home?"

"You will have to drive by yourself. I will pay you. I can't afford to let anyone leave right now. Don't forget, you have an open invitation to the yacht. Thanks again for making it look so good."

Episode 5

"Iris!" the captain yelled. "You cannot invite anyone you want to my yacht. I don't like Rocco's friends any more than I like him."

"I invited him because he is doing me a favor and bringing the Rolls up to our standards."

"The man works with his hands. What the blooming hell is wrong with you? He is inferior to us," the captain hollered at Iris.

Iris was steaming. She was in the process of either walking away or taking him on in mortal combat.

"Penny," she shouted, "you have not been paying the bills properly. Furthermore, you have been spending business funds for your own fun."

"I need to have fun just like anyone else on board," he replied. "It's is my yacht after all."

"You signed a note with me. We are using the yacht as collateral. I'm calling the note. Now I'm in charge," she said. "I'm taking over your state room. You may have my suite."

The captain wasn't too sure what the hell just happened. He was shaking and about to faint. "Are you all right?" she asked.

Pendleton went down and woke up in the hospital three days later. The complete crew was in the room, talking and laughing. Iris was upset with herself for causing his mental breakdown even though the queen actually started it months earlier. "Where am I?" he cried.

"Hi, Penny dear. How are you feeling?" asked Deana.

"I'm dizzy. Where the blue blazes am I?"

Rocco stepped up to the bed. "You are in the hospital, cry baby."

"Oh, Penny, how are you?" asked Billie Joe. "You look so white. Are you sure you are all right?"

"No, I'm not all right. I want to get out of here now. Somebody get my uniform immediately," he ordered.

At this time, the nurse entered the room. "What are all you people doing here? Clear out. He needs some more rest," she yelled as she pulled out a giant needle.

"You're not going to stick me with that," he yelled.

"Oh yes, I am," she yelled back at him.

"Excuse me, nurse," interrupted Rocco, "if you want, I will hold him down for you."

"Yes, that would be quite helpful," she replied.

"No way. I don't want that blooming grease ball to touch me," Pendleton screamed.

"Hey," replied the nurse, "I'm Italian too. Try this for grease." She stabbed him in the ass with the needle.

Rocco was now laughing so loud that every one outside the room rushed back in to see the captain with a big needle sticking out of his ass.

"Look," cried Billie Joe, "he has dimples."

"Cover him up," Deana yelled. "He will get a cold."

Pendleton was now out cold. The needle had a sedative in it.

"Let's go back to the boat," said Iris.

"No, this is too much fun," replied Rocco.

"Come on, Rock," replies Olga. "We will stop at redneck bar, yeah?"

"Sure, let's go," he answered.

"Come on, girls. Let's go to Booties for a stiff one," Iris said.

******

A week later, the captain who was now the ex-captain, was back aboard the yacht. He was relocated between Rocco and Olga's cabins. In Iris's old room.

"Rock, you want to make captain crazy?" exclaimed Olga.

"What do you have in mind, Olga?" replied Rocco. "Wait a minute, I know what to do."

"Yeah?" grunted Olga.

"Yeah," answered Rocco. "We will steal his girly shoes and give them to the dancers at the club."

"Yeah, good thing to do," she replied.

"Come on, Olga," he said. "We can get in there now. He is out somewhere."

Rocco stole Pendleton's high heels and was going to sell them to the dancers to get on the good side of them for a little action. Olga returned to the Rocco's room to lift weights. She has lost weight and pumped up her body.

"Olga, where are you?" hollered Billie Joe. "I have time to teach you how to do your makeup right now."

Billie Joe promised to help her learn how to do makeup. She couldn't find her in the kitchen, so she looked in Rocco's room.

"Here you are," Billie said.

"Yeah, I make body strong. Rocco likes strong body. You like strong body?"

Billie was amazed at her muscles. "To tell you the truth, Olga, I don't think women should be to muscular. It makes them look less feminine."

"I look pretty, Rock says."

"Honey, when we do your makeup, you will be beautiful," replied Billie.

"When do we do that?"

"I have time now. Why don't you put that two-hundred-pound pile of iron on the floor, and we can start now. Let's go into your room. What I'm going to do is teach you so you can do it anytime you need to."

"Yeah, I need to make Tyler the bartender happy for me."

"Tyler," she answered.

"Wow, he is a handsome man."

Olga glanced at Billie Joe. "I like his tan. He is a hero bronze statue in Russia."

Billie Joe soon has Olga looking good.

"Olga," she said. "You have to shave your legs. They look awful with all that black hair growing on them."

"They like hairy legs in Russia. It's very romantic to have hairy armpits also in my homeland."

"Are you kidding or what?" replied Billie.

"I not kid you, Billie," Olga answered.

"Olga, if you don't want to upset Tyler. You must either shave your legs or wear opaque stockings."

"What is this word *opaque*?" she asked.

"It means you can't see through them. He won't be able to see all that black hair."

"People see through my legs?"

"No, Olga. They see through your stockings to view the hair on your legs."

"I don't want stockings. Tyler will like hair just like Rock likes."

"Okay, Olga, you win." Billie Joe sighed. In an attempt to change the subject, Billie asked,

"Olga who is this picture of?" "Gorbachev is man in frame," she answered. "He makes Russia free like here." She smiled with satisfaction.

"Who is this other man, Olga?"

"No good pig. Head of KBG. Putin is good dartboard. See holes in head."

"Olga, aren't you worried that they will come to get you?"

"No worry, Billie Joe."

"Hey, Olga, I have a gift for you. It will give you something to aspire to. It's a picture of Marilyn Munroe and a doll of her too."

Olga examined the picture for a short time, then asked, "Who is Marilyn?"

"She was a big movie star." Billie paused, then lied to Olga to make her feel good about herself. "Who looked a lot like you."

"I movie star," Olga repeated.

******

The captain by now has returned to his room and discovered his high heels are gone. Rocco was his first thought.

That little grease ball bastard. I still have the keys to the rooms. I'll look there first, he thought.

After rummaging through Rocco's room and finding nothing, he stopped to think. "Olga!" he exclaimed. *She must have them. I'll check her out next.*

He entered her room only to find the picture of Marilyn next to the puppet. As he exited the room, his coat was bulging with stolen goods from her room.

Olga passed him in the hall and saw the bulging jacket.

She entered her room and noticed the puppet and the picture are missing. "My stuff!" she yelled as she headed back out the door to find him.

Olga headed straight for his room. She stood outside for a minute, deciding what to do. She suddenly kicked the door open with her size 12 right foot. She caught Pendleton changing into his favorite dress.

"I'll make a man out of captain," she hollered.

The captain turned to face her. His bra was hanging from one arm. His skirt was askew as he was trying to zipper it up.

"What the hell are you doing here in my room? Leave immediately!" he screamed.

"I take doll," she said as she looked at his well-endowed body. "You take stuff. I fix you."

"You stole my shoes!" he hollered back at her.

Olga chased him around the room a few times, finally catching him near the bed. She grabbed him by the head and picked him up off his feet. Her next move was to raise him over her head. She placed her other hand between his legs and lifted.

"You're fired," he yelled. "Get your hand away from my thing!" Because the ceiling was low and Olga was so big, he hit the roof. "Put me down you bloody lunatic!" he screamed in total panic.

She threw him on the bed, looked at him, then dove on top of him. "You're smothering me!" he yelled.

The sound was muffled by Olga's big body. She started making out with him. Big very wet kisses. All the time, she was saying, "I be movie star."

"Ah," coughed the captain. "Get the blooming love of England off me." He struggled to get out from under her, but she was too strong and heavy.

Olga kissed him all over his face. It was like a 150-pound Newfoundland dog drooling on his face. She then reached down, pulled up his skirt, and tore down on his undies. She grabbed his manly parts. The captain was screaming. He was squirming so hard he pulled a muscle in his back.

"I'm being raped. Your breath is terrible. For the love of England, I'm being raped. Somebody get this stinky gorilla off me."

He was on the bottom, trapped by Olga, and she wasn't about to let him up.

"I give treatment to you. Not to steal stuff."

Olga was pissed, and the captain was going to know it when she was done with him.

"I fix," she said. Thinking she had finished with him, she started to pull his undies up, then started to laugh. She laughed so hard at him that she sneezed.

"Ahhh!" he yelled as her fluids hit him in the face. "You have poisoned me with your snots, you filthy pig. God bless the queen. Somebody help me!" Olga was tired of his whimpering. She punched him and knocked him out. "You sleep now," she said and grabbed her stuff, then left his room.

******

Rocco was in his room, lifting weights, when Olga arrived. She looked flustered.

"Captain steal things."

She grunted as she laid her doll on the bed to join Rocco in weight lifting.

"What?" Rocco hissed. "I knew someone was in my room. It must have been him."

"Yeah, he look for shoes."

"Where is he now?" asked Rocco.

"Sleeping in room," she answered with a mischievous smirk.

"I'll fix him," replied Rocco.

"I help," answered Olga.

"Let's go," Rocco said as he put on his shirt, then opened the door to the hall.

"I come quick also," Olga answered.

The animal society was hiding under Rocco's bed.

"We should go too," said Maxi.

"Yes," replied Robin. "We will meet you there. Batman and I have to take the secret route."

"Okay" answered José. "We can meet you but be quick. It might all be over by the time you get there."

"Don't worry, we will make it on time for the fun," answered Batman.

"Where is Coco?" asked Maxi.

"I'm over here," Coco answered with a slurred voice. "I'll pass. I'm not up to running around just to watch that nitwit captain get a beaten from Rocco."

"By Coco," said José

The mice had already headed out to watch Rocco and Olga take care of the captain. They had to cover more distance on shorter legs.

The mice arrived a minute before José and Maxi. The cabin door was open. It had a big footprint on it.

"José, look at the door. That foot print is big. It can only belong to Olga."

"Yes, I agree," replied Batman. "It's bigger than me and you put together Robin."

"All right, all right," cried Maxi. "Let's quiet down and get in the room to see what's going on."

"I hear them talking. It sounds like Rocco," replied José.

"Olga, after you get his clothing off, grab his feet and help me drag him outside."

"I take clothes," she replied.

"Now put him back on the bed for a moment," said Rocco "See if you can find some tape."

"No find tape but lipstick is here," replied Olga.

"That will do," answered Rocco.

"Let's get him up on deck behind the cabin, so no one will find him."

They rapped him up in a sheet and brought the captain up to the deck. Rocco cut a hole in the sheet all around his butt so the sun would give him some blisters, and he wouldn't be able to sit down for a few days. He groaned, and Olga punched him again.

"He sleep some more," she announced.

"Good girl, but next time, let me hit him."

"Rock, I have idea," Olga said. "You roll him over."

"I want his ass to burn," replied Rocco.

"Yeah," answered Olga. "First, I decorate face."

They rolled him over on his back, and Olga wrote with lipstick on his forehead. "Rock, how do you right *dickhead* in English."

"Do it in Russian," he answered.

"Yeah, I can do Russian," she replied.

"I get it," answered Rocco. "He will wipe off the lipstick and the skin under it will be white. That's great, Olga. People will see it and ask what it means. The dickhead won't know because he can't read Russian."

"Yeah." She started to laugh. "He will be dickhead."

They both started to laugh, and the animals joined in.

"Did you hear someone?" asked Rocco.

"Yeah,"

"Be quiet, you guys," whispered Maxi. "They can hear us."

"No way," José said. "The humans can't hear us."

A deep sleepy sounding voice came from under the lifeboat.

"Well, I know one who can. He used to be dickheads butler. He could converse with me," hissed Coco. "What the hell is all this noise about? Don't you fools know I'm sleeping?"

"We aren't making the noise," replied José. "It's the humans."

"Well, whoever it is had better quiet down. I have a hangover. My head is killing me. I'll scratch out the eyes of anyone who disturbs me again."

Robin, in an effort to get on the good side of the cat, cut in to the conversation.

"We can get you an aspirin, if you like, Coco."

"Go away, all of you. I'll just have a drink that will fix it."

Maxi glanced around at the others. "I think we have to get Coco to Alcoholics Anonymous."

"I'm not going to any club like that. Who will pay for this treatment?"

"It's free, Coco. We can do the taxi cab thing again."

"Well, I'll have to think about it," Coco replied.

"Great Caesar's ghost, what's to think about?" replied José.

"Olga, get the duct tape. We have to keep the sheet on him, so the rest of his body won't burn."

"Yeah, we tape feet?"

"Good idea, then tape him to the rail, so he can't escape. Put some tape on his mouth too. He will be screaming like a little girl when he wakes up this time."

"Come on, Coco. Come with us to a meeting. You will be happy if you stop drinking," Maxi encouraged.

"They have free donuts there, Robin, and I use to live under the stairs at one of the meeting places.

"Yuck, donuts." The cat made a face as though it was poison. "Now I know I'm not going,"
         replied Coco.

"Olga, let's get out of here before he comes to again," whispered Rocco.

******

Three o'clock that afternoon, Iris was in control of the monthly staff meeting. The entire crew was present and enjoying sandwiches and homemade brew. Iris was trying to get the meeting started, but Pendleton was missing.

"I say we have a bit of a problem. Has anyone seen the captain?" Iris asked.

Rocco and Olga were in the rear of the group, giggling. Billie Joe and Deana were chatting.

"I guess no one cares about Penny," Iris said in a way that's more of a question.

"I saw him this morning," Rocco answered.

"Well," Iris said, "we will have to start without him. Let it be known that in the future when I call a meeting, I expect everyone to attend."

"Everyone is here," called out Rocco. "Pendleton doesn't count anyway."

"Rocco, he is my brother. I will thank you to have respect for the family that pays you."

"Yes, you're right, Iris. How about we send José to look for him?"

"No, let's start the meeting. He will show up sooner or later."

The words had no sooner come out of her mouth when a loud thump was heard. "I'll kill that friggin grease ball this time!"

"Penny, is that you?" called Iris.

She received no answer, so she called out again. "Penny, is that you, dear?"

Deana, now alarmed, joined her.

"Penny dear, where are you? Come and join us."

Rocco and Olga were almost laughing out loud. They were trying to hide it and not doing so very well.

"Where the hell are they?" someone yelled from the other side of the cabin. "I'm going to kill the both of them!" "Penny, we're over here, dear. Please join us," replied Deana.

"I'll join you all right. Just wait till I get my hands on the blooming pair of them."

At this point, Iris got up to fetch him. He appeared from around the corner at the same instant. Everyone stood when they saw him. Rocco broke the ice.

"Hey, Captain," he yelled, "this isn't a toga party."

"Yeah" joined in Olga. "You need uniform."

The animal society was having their monthly meeting under the couch. Robin glanced at the captain and said. "Oh fuck."

José turned, then yelled, "Great Caesar's ghost, what the hell is that?"

Maxi looked at the others, then said, "He looks funnier than a cockatoo's ass!"

Batman said, "Let's get the hell out of here before he starts shooting."

Pendleton looked at Olga and started screaming at her. Olga stood up, and the captain backed off.

"I'm going to get my gun," he yelled as he glanced at Rocco.

Rocco stood up also. "What does that writing on your forehead say?"

"What writing?" asked the captain.

"The lipstick, dear," answered Deana.

"What lipstick are you talking about?" he snapped.

"Penny," Iris asked, "where were you, and who wrote on your forehead?"

Pendleton was becoming more enraged. He looked at his reflection in the window and howled.

"You overgrown Russian whore! You did this!"

Olga didn't like his choice of words and stepped toward him one giant step at a time. "You talk to me?" she asked in a menacing voice.

"Yes, I'm talking to you and that greasy rat friend of yours. I know he had something to do with this."

Now Rocco advanced toward him in a menacing way.

"You talking to me?" he asked, his Boston accent sounding more like Brooklyn.

Iris could take no more. "Will somebody tell me what in the name of the blooming queen is going on here?"

"These two tied me up and did this to me," screamed the captain.

"We didn't touch him!" Rocco yelled back.

"He paranoid," answered Olga.

"I'm not paranoid," screamed the captain.

"No, you are. You're nuts," answered Rocco.

Billie Joe, who was still in shock and trying to figure out what had happened, asked, "Captain, what does the lipstick say?"

"I don't know. It is strange-looking writing."

"It say dickhead," answered Olga, thereby confirming she had something to do with it.

"Olga, how do you know what it says?" asked Iris.

Rocco joined in and yelled out, "It's Russian writing, but she didn't do it. She was with me lifting weights when it happened."

"How do you know when it happened?" asked Deana.

"I'm guessing," replied Rocco.

The captain was getting tired of the whole mess and decided to sit for the rest of the argument and have a drink. He planted his butt on the deck chair rather hard.

"Ahhh." He let out a sound like a girl delivering a child. It sounded like he was being tortured.

He jumped up and started yelling.

"Somebody throw cold water on it! Somebody throw water on it!" No one knew what he meant until he started running away from them. They all saw his little white ass burnt bright red on each cheek at the same time.

"I'll help," cried Billie Joe as she threw her homemade booze on his butt.

"Ahhh!" he screamed again as he ran in circles. "You dumb hill-billy. That was pure alcohol, it stings to high heaven."

"I'm not as dumb as you look right now," she hollered back at him.

Iris finally interceded, "Penny, why don't you and Deana go to your room and take care of this mess before anyone else gets hurt.

"I'm going, but you two haven't heard the end of this," he hissed and pointed at Olga and Rocco. "I guarantee you."

"See ya," replied Rocco.

"Be-bye," replied Olga.

"Come, Penny. I'll take care of you," Deana said as she helped him out of the room by his toga.

When they got to his cabin, she told him to lie on his stomach. "I'll rub some lotion on your bum dear."

"Pease be careful, sweetie. Don't hurt me. You know how delicate I am."

"Yes, dear, don't worry. I'll put some bandage on over the lotion."

"Deana, whatever you're doing, it's getting me excited. Do you think we could roll around when you're done?"

"Oh, darling, I would love to," Deana answered.

"Oh boy," the captain replied. "Hurry, dear, I can't wait any longer."

"I'm all done, Penny. Here comes your treat," she whispered.

"Yes, dear, I'm ready."

Deana climbed on top of him with a bump and a grind. All was silent for about one second.

"Ahhh!" cried the captain, quite obviously in pain. "Get the bloody hell off me. My ass is burning like a knife from hell just penetrated it."

"Sorry, dear. I didn't think it would still hurt with all the cream on it!"

"You didn't think at all, you blithering idiot," he replied.

"You have no right to talk to me that way, you fool," she yelled back at him.

"I have all the right. I am the captain!" he cried, his voice in anguish from his butt pain.

"I'll show you who is right," Deana screamed at him. "I put this bandage on, and now, I will take it off.""No, don't touch me," he blurted out, still in pain. Deana deftly rolled him on to his stomach.

"How does it feel, dear, to have a blithering idiot for a nurse?" she hissed.

"I call this instant electrolysis."

She then ripped the bandage off as slow as she could. "Dear, it's free. Most nurses get fifty dollars per hour."

"My god," he cried, "what have you done to my ass? I can't feel it anymore. I think I'm going to faint."

And he did.

Deana put some pepper on the bum and replaced the bandage.

She left his cabin. A smile crossed her lips. Deana was more upset at Pendleton than ever before. He had insulted her, and she retaliated. Penny would feel her wrath for a week if he didn't find the pepper on his butt.

"Hi, Deana. Where is my brother?" asked Iris with a smile.

"He's resting in his cabin," she replied.

"I think I'll bring him something nice to eat and drink. I can't believe what Rocco and Olga did to him. Maybe it is time to let them two go. What they did was very mean." Iris sighed.

"I'm very upset at your brother. He called me a nitwit."

"Wow, that's very unlike him, Deana. Why did he do that?"

"Well, I was helping him with his butt, and he wanted sex. Then he got mad at me when I tried to please him."

"I'm sad to hear that, Deana. He is usually so gentle."

"Yes, you're right, Iris. It must have been the sunburn that caused all the trouble. I have to go back to him and make amends."

"Good idea, Deana. I'll go with you," answered Iris. "Good, let's go."

The two ladies returned to the captain's room. They knocked three times on the green door. No one answered. Deana, fearing the worst, opened the door.

"Penny, what are you doing?" she whispered.

"Deana," replied Iris, "it's pretty obvious what he's doing. Self pleasure is so vile. He's fine. Let's go." Iris slammed the door.

"Yes," answered Deana. "Let's go."

Episode 6

"I called this meeting to update everyone on the goings-on aboard ship," said Iris. "The first thing is an update on the Rolls. Luke says he is almost done. He is waiting for parts for the interior. The next thing is the tug of war. Olga will represent us in the games. Rocco, it will be your duty to help Olga get ready."

Rocco stood up. "I don't have time for this. I have to cook. When will I find time?"

"You find time to sex me," cried Olga

"That's different!" snapped Rocco.

"Rocco," Iris said, "you are in charge of her training, and that's that."

Olga had something to say. "Iris, I need Rock, but I don't want to bother him. I make strong on own."

Rocco answered her, "Olga, don't worry. I'll help you get strong. You'll be the strongest woman in the world."

"Well," replied Iris, "that's settled. Now the next thing is the brochure. How are you girls doing on that?"

"We are all set, Iris," Billie Joe answered.

Iris looked around, then continued the meeting.

"Where is my brother? Has anyone seen him?" She paused and glanced at Rocco and Olga. "You two go find him and don't hurt him anymore."

"I'm not his keeper," replied Rocco. "Someone else can find him."

"I find," said Olga.

"Very well," replied Iris. "Deana, I want a copy of the brochure so I can read it before it is printed." Iris stood up and signaled the end of the meeting. "We are all done for now. Are there any questions?"

"I have a question," answered Billie Joe "When is the Rolls coming back, and when is the tug of war going to take place?"

"The Rolls will return next week. I'm glad that you ask. I'm looking for volunteers to go pick it up at Luke's shop. Anyone interested?"

"I'll go," answered Rocco. "I live there. It will be like a vacation."

"Me too," replied Billie Joe. "I always wanted to see Boston up close."

"Count me in," said Deana. "I want to see the freedom trail."

"Oh good," replied Iris. "I am happy to see you folks sticking together. I will pay for everything, so consider it a vacation. Luke fixed the Rolls up for cheap, so I have money left over."

"Does that mean we can fly first class?" asked Rocco.

"I want to take the train," said Billie Joe.

"I'll call the airport and get tickets for us," answered Deana.

The animal society sat quietly under the couch, listening to the people. "I want to go with them!" cried José.

"No, José, stay with us," answered Maxi.

"That could be dangerous," added Robin.

"No, Boston is nice and safe," added Batman.

"I'm not afraid. The humans will help me." José grinned.

"Well, you had better snuggle up to Deana. She is ordering tickets," squawked Maxi. "I'll help. Watch this."

Maxi strutted out to the open deck and flew over to Deana's shoulder. "Take, José," she squawked. "José wants to go to Boston."

Deana looked at the bird and smiled.

"Yes, Maxi, that's a good idea. I'll sign him up for a ride under the airline seat. He will keep everyone happy when we get tired and bitchy."

"Thank you, honey. You are beautiful," replied Maxi.

"He did it!" cried Batman.

"Yeah!" answered Robin. "But I would rather see the cat go for a long one-way ride instead."

"Well, I'm happy," said José. "I'm going on vacation with the girls. It will be fun."

The flight to Boston was uneventful. The dog was loved by everyone that had a chance to see him. They were picked up by Luke in the Rolls. Rocco insisted that they go straight to Revere Beach to drink with his buddies. Luke already had reservations at one of the better East Boston restaurants, which was just a few minutes from the airport.

"Luke," Rocco asked, "where are we going to eat? I'm starved."

"It's a new place. You haven't been barred from there yet," answered Luke as he tried not to laugh at the thought of Rocco making it through dinner without trouble.

"What kind of food is it?" asked Billie Joe.

"Italian," answered Luke.

"Great," added Deana. "I love Italian food. Is it a good chef, Luke?"

"You'll see. We will be there in a minute."

They enjoyed their meal. Rocco behaved, and they headed for Winthrop for a rest. They would leave in two days for Florida to bring the Rolls back.

"Rocco, why don't you show us around?" asked Deana.

"Count me out," replied Luke.

"I'll go," said Billie Joe.

"Luke, take the dog home with you," Rocco said. "We will be out late. I'm going to get drunk with these two."

"Rock, be careful," Luke warned. "The cops are everywhere these days, and most of them already know you."

"Don't worry, I'll outrun them," he answered.

"You're not using my car. You better rent one for the night."

"Come on, Luke. Let me use the car."

"Not a chance, my friend."

Billie Joe entered the conversation.

"I know what to do. We will use the Rolls."

"I'll be the designated driver."

"That's fine with me," replied Luke. "Iris will have you killed if you scratch it, and I'm not going to fix it again."

"Jolly good," replied Rocco. "Drop us off at the garage, and we will pick it up.

"Jolly good." Luke laughed. "What are you an Italian English man?"

"I picked that up from Pendleton the dip shit," replied Rocco.

"All right," answered Luke. They had parked beside the Rolls. "Here is the Rolls. Have fun."

"Luke, you should come with us. We will pay for your drinks. We're using Iris's money,"

Deana whispered.

"No, my wife will kill me. The last time I did that, she ran me over with her Yolks wagon beetle."

"Did you get hurt?" asked Billie Joe.

"Not till I got home. Then, she really got upset."

"Well, I'm jolly glad to see you survived." Rocco laughed.

"Hey, goomba, don't scratch that car. I broke my ass on the finish," replied Luke.

"See ya, Luke. Have a jolly good blooming time at home," Rocco said as he laughed all the way to the Rolls.

The three of them entered the car and started the engine. It roared to life, then the lights came on. The vehicle looked great, and Rock was the pilot in charge of this flying carpet. They headed out to find some of Rock's old friends at the local watering holes. He took them to Revere Beach, which used to be a giant amusement park, now diminished to just a few lounges. After a long night of Rocco's war stories, they finally arrived at the motel reserved for them by Iris. Rocco went in for the key, and five minutes later, the Revere Police arrived.

"Deana, do you think Rocco said something to the attendant?"

"No, Billie. I *know* he said something stupid. He can't let anything go. He has to react to everything."

"Let's go in, get the key, and see what is going on," replied Billie Joe. They entered the door just as Rocco was escorted out by the two cops. "Rocco, what happened?" asked Billie Joe.

"He's barred from here forever, and if you two are with him, you are also," replied the cop.

"I didn't do anything," Rocco replied.

"Rock, you must have done something," answered Deana. "We don't have a room to sleep in now. What should we do?"

"We can go to Luke's house and sleep there. I'll call him. Let's go in that direction for now."

"Why don't we just head south to Florida and find another motel on the way?" Billie Joe said.

"Luke has José. We have to go there anyway, so let's see if we can sleep there. We have nothing to lose," replied Deana.

"Luke says we can't sleep there. His dogs will go nuts all night. We'll just get José and leave for the boat."

"I'll drive," said Billie Joe, "until you two sober up. After we get José, you two go to sleep for a couple of hours.

"All right, let's go home," replied Deana.

"I am home," said Rocco.

"Thanks to you, none of us are home," answered Billie Joe.

"No more sex for you when we tell Olga what you did." Deana laughed.

"Don't tell Olga anything," replied Rocco.

The two girls started chanting at Rocco.

"Rocco has a girlfriend. Rocco has a girlfriend." They broke into wild laughter. The two girls giggled for about a half hour. Rocco was upset and wouldn't speak to them until they got to Georgia. It would have been better if he didn't open his mouth at all because it was while talking to a local cop who was giving them a ticket for speeding that he decided to speak.

"Good morning," said the patrolman. "My name is Aleutian P. Pearpecker. I am a police officer representing the town of Pigs Hollow in the beautiful state of Georgia." He paused as he studied the Rolls and three of them now in need of freshening up. Rocco busted out laughing at the cop's name.

"Ya'll think this is funny, son?" the cop asked.

He was not quite understanding why Rocco was laughing.

"What did you say your name was again?" asked Rocco. He was now laughing so hard that he was almost unable to speak.

"Ya'll been drinking or smoking some of that funny weed?"

"No, of course not," replied Rocco.

"I don't drink."

"What you laughing at boy?"

"I'm laughing at your name. It sounds gay, doesn't it?"

The cop's face was turning the third shade of red.

"Ya'll been driving at a high rate of speed. Why, you must have been close to ninety miles per hour 'cording to my radar," the cop hissed.

"You can't give us a ticket," Rocco yelled back at him. "We were going the same speed as the other cars."

The cop moved back from the window and pulled out his night stick to answer Rocco.

"Ya'll listen to me, Yankee boy. I'm making the decisions here. Ya'll keep yapping, and you be going to my jail, boy."

"You can't put us in jail for talking," Rocco answered in a very defiant voice.

"Ya'll bringing me to the boiling point, boy."

"Officer, we apologize," sang out Billie Joe.

The cop was still addressing Rocco.

"You had best shut up, Yankee boy. 'Fore I really get angry."

He turned to the girls.

"You are a pretty one," he said to Billie Joe. "Your apology is accepted."

"Oh, thank you, Officer," Deana said from the backseat. "Is it all right if we let the dog out to pee while you finish the ticket?"

"Yes, it is," he replied in a very strong Southern drawl. "See if ya'll can keep that other puppy under control also."

"What other puppy?"

"That ratty-looking chauffeur in the front seat."

"Yes, Officer," replied Billie Joe. "He will be quiet. Thank you."

José by now was getting annoyed by the cop also.

The cop continued to write the ticket while the girls tried to calm Rocco down.

"Rock, you have to keep quiet, or we will all get arrested," said Billie Joe.

"The cop is a jerk rebel. He called me a chauffeur. I'm a citizen," replied Rocco.

"Shush, he will hear you."

"Who cares?" replied Rocco. "Look at him. He weighs three hundred pounds. He can hardly walk. I'll kick his ass for him."

As the three talked, they heard the cop yelling at José. "You son of a bitch, dog. I ought to shoot you," he hollered. "That does it. You three Yankees going to jail now.

"What happened?" asked Deana.

"Ya'll have a very vicious mutt here. He urinated on my new shoe. I spent all night polishing it."

"You only polished one shoe?" replied Billie Joe. "That's dumb."

"Big deal," yelled Rocco "We have been here for a half hour waiting for you to write out a simple ticket. You can write, I hope."

"I'll show you how good I write," replied the cop. "Get out off that vehicle. You're going to jail for rude and disorderly conduct, interfering with a officer in the line of duty, speeding beyond the normal limits, peeing on my foot, driving a stolen vehicle, and being Italian."

"Listen, you fat rebel pig! I'll kick your ass before I go to jail!" Rocco yelled at the cop. He jumped out of the car with the two girls holding on to him. The cop hit him with his club, and Rock went down for the count.

"Now, I'm adding assaulting a police officer to the list," whispered the cop.

"Officer, you killed him!" cried Deana. "No, ma'am, he's just faking it. He doesn't want to get a taste of Southern hospitality. Now if you two ladies will step out of the vehicle. I'll place you under arrest also."

"You can't arrest us. We didn't do anything!" yelled Billie Joe.

"I'm arresting you for being with these two Yankees. You're a Southern bell. You should know better."

He looked at Deana.

"I'm arresting you for being in a stolen car and aiding and abetting a criminal chauffeur."

The cop smiled at the thought of being clever about the chauffeur part. He handcuffed Rocco. Two more local cops pulled up to help. They handcuffed each of the girls and put each one in a separate car. José went with Rocco. He was considered a criminal also.

"What about our car?" asked Deana.

"It's not your car. It's stolen and will be impounded. Ya'll don't have any right to it. I might take it for myself."

"Yes, Officer, you are correct. The blooming thing belongs to our boss. We are to bring it home to Florida. We didn't know that we didn't have the papers," replied Deana.

"Ya'll best hope your boss can back you up, or ya'll be going to prison. The chain gang, I think."

The cop chuckled, then told the other two to take all to jail.

******

They arrived at the jail and were loaded into the cell. Rocco finally woke up. Deana had torn a piece off her blouse to bandage his head. He had a small cut but nothing much more important.

"What happened?" asked Rocco.

"You lost another fight and got us all arrested," answered Billie Joe.

"It wasn't my fault. Don't blame me. It was José that did it."

"Rock, it really doesn't matter now. We have to get a lawyer when we get our one telephone call. I'll call Iris and tell her to get us a lawyer. You call a bail bonds man. Deana, you call Pendleton in case I don't reach Iris."

"Good thinking," replied Deana.

"That fat rebel needs a good beating," mumbled Rocco.

"You lost the last blooming round. Let it go. We are in enough trouble. They have a list of charges a mile long against you."

"Deana, I have an idea," said Billie Joe. "We are pretty females. Why

don't we turn on the charm? Maybe they will let us go and only arrest Rocco."

"Hey!" Rocco said.

"You can't leave me here all alone."

"You won't be alone. José is under arrest also," replied Deana.

Later that day, the police chief came in to interview them. Deana and Billie Joe had enough time to fix their makeup and were looking good.

When the chief walked in and saw them, he stopped in his tracks and smiled. It was more of a shit-eating grin. The girls turned on the charm. Billie Joe got her best Southern accent back just in time.

"Afternoon, ladies. I'm Chief T. Darrel Willfart. You folks in a whole bunch of trouble."

"Afternoon, Chief. Ya'll looking very nice in that uniform," Billie Joe said with a big, big smile.

"Why thank you. You're a Southern belle. You shouldn't be in jail. Maybe we can work something out," he replied.

"Why, Officer," said Deana, "your offering us a chance to leave?"

"Well, you're a fine-looking lady also," the chief answered with his grin going full force. "Where ya'll from, miss?"

"England, but now I live in Florida," she answered.

"Well, you girls seem to be okay, but your chauffeur is in serious trouble. We just added another crime to the list of offenses he has committed in the beautiful state of Georgia.

"Oh no," replied Deana.

"Ya'll going to tell us what that charge will be?" asked Billie Joe.

"Yes, I will, miss. What is you nickname?"

"Why, Chief, ya'll can call me Billie."

"Billie, that's a pretty name. Your chauffeur Rocco was transporting moonshine over the state line. I will have to call the Feds."

Deana and Billie looked at each other.

"We have to have a private talk, Chief. Would we be able to go outside?"

"Ladies, you two can go anyplace you want. You are hereby released. Perhaps we can have lunch together?"

"Sure, Chief. What's your nickname? We don't want to call you Chief all day."

"Ya'll can call me Theodore."

"Theodore, what a nice manly name you have. Theodore, we will meet you at the restaurant."

"Okay, it's the only one in town. You can't miss it. It's called The Last Raccoon. Tell Ms. Maybell that you are with me. She will give you a window seat."

The chief smiled as he pictured a double header with the girls after he got them drunk.

"Sure thing, Theodore," replied Deana in a sexy voice.

Billie Joe was in deep thought. She knew they couldn't let Rocco take the blame for the beer.

"Deana, we have to rescue Rocco from jail," urged Billie Joe.

"Yes, I know, but what can we do?"

"Maybe if we have sex with the chief, we can soften him up. What do you think?"

"I'm not going to touch that man," replied Deana. "It's your booze. You have to do the dirty work, not me."

"Okay. Let's go to lunch. I'll flirt with him and see what I can do to get Rocco out of jail."

"Billie, be careful. We are in a scary situation. There is no telling what he has in mind for us."

"He is a Southern gentleman. Don't worry so much. I trust him," replied Billie Joe. "Let's go to lunch with him and find out."

"I think I'll go visit Rocco. You can be alone with him that way. All right?"

"Sure, Deana. I'll catch up with you later and let you know what happens."

"Good luck. I hope you succeed and get Rock out of jail," answered Deana as she headed for the jail.

******

"Hi, Theodore. I'm so happy you could make it to lunch with me. It's always nice when two Southerners can get together."

"Yes, my little Southern belle, I agree. Let's have a drink before lunch and get to know each other better. Where is your friend Deana? I was looking forward to being with her."

"She went to visit Rocco."

"He's in a lot of trouble especially, with the illegal booze we found in that stolen vehicle."

"Theodore, the Rolls is not stolen. It belongs to my boss. She had us pick it up in Boston and bring it home to Florida."

"Well, that might be true. We haven't heard from your contact Ms. Iris, ma'am. Until we clear that issue up, it's stolen. Now what would you like for a drink my dear?" asked the chief.

"I really would like a drink of my moonshine," replied Billie Joe.

"Did you say your moonshine?" replied the chief.

"Yes, Chief, I'm sorry but that belongs to me, not Rocco. I can't let him take the blame."

"Why, Billie Joe," replied the chief in a sympathetic voice. "How did you learn to make such good stuff?"

"My grand pappy showed me and my paw the formula a long time ago."

"Who in the world is your granddaddy?"

"Well, he was the best bootlegger that ever lived. That's who he was," she replied.

"I guess you are correct judging from the taste young lady, but what was his name?"

"Theodore, do you think we can get some of my stuff delivered here?"

"Why, yes, my sweet little dumpling, we sure can."

The chief picked up his radio and told the sergeant at the desk to send him a bottle of evidence from the Rolls-Royce. Within a couple of minutes, a police car pulled up outside, and an officer of the law brought a bottle of booze to them.

"Here, my sweet one, you can do the honors and pour us a stiff one to start."

"Why, thank you, Theodore. I will be happy to help out."

"Now, tell me, Billie Joe. What is your grandpappy's name?"

"Grandpappy is still alive. You have to promise that you won't arrest him. Do you?"

"Why, yes, I promise not to arrest him. After all, my grand-pappy was a top-notch moonshiner too. Why, legend has it that there was only one man better, and that was Elmer J. Fuddle. He resided in Sleeping Hollow. As I remember, it was a town in South Carolina over near that south of the border place."

"Oh my," replied Billie Joe. "My last name is Fuddle. My grand-pappy is a Fuddle also. Do you think he is the one? He did live in South Carolina, and as I heard it, he was the best there ever was."

"Well, I'll be darned. I have in front of me the granddaughter of the most famous moonshiner that ever there was."

"Well, isn't this something?" Billie Joe said. "Let's have another drink."

"Now go easy on there that stuff, young lady. It's mighty powerful."

"I been drinking this here stuff since I was a little one. No higher than a Pekingese puppy dog," she replied.

"A Pekingese what?" he asked.

"Never mind, Chief, about the dog. I need to find a way to help Rocco get out of jail. Did you know he is a jack of all trades and the best Italian cook that ever lived?"

"He's a cook? Well, that's good. I'll get him a job cooking at the restaurant while he awaits his trial. We can't hang him for running illegal booze, but he is guilty of all the other things on the list, I'm sure of that."

"Oh, thank you, Chief. Does that mean you won't put me in jail for making moonshine either?"

"That's right, little lady. You will have to give me the recipe for the moonshine though."

"Theodore, I promised my grand pappy that I wouldn't ever do that."

"Well, a promise is a promise, so maybe I can work something out with my paw, the judge."

"That would be nice if you can get Rocco out of jail. I will do anything you want except give up the recipe."

"Anything? Why, I'll have to take you up on that later, but right now, I think we should celebrate the rediscovery of the formula to the best moonshine ever to come out of the South. Let's have and other drink. Only this time, I'm going to have Maybell mix some fruit juice with it."

"Glorious, Chief, that would be fine with me. I could drink this stuff all day long. How 'bout you?"

"No, thanks. This is starting to get to me," he replied.

"Why, Theodore, do ya'll mean to tell me ya can't handle your liquor?"

"I got to go see Pa right now and get your friend out of jail. When I tell Pa about the formula, he will be very happy to help you."

"I will be at the jail visiting Rocco. Let me know, please?"

"Yes, ma'am, I will do just that," he said.

The chief looked at her, then got up and fell down. She helped him up, and he staggered out the front door. Two of his officers helped him into the car, and they were off. Billie Joe was hardly fazed and walked over to the jail to give Rocco the good news.

The next day, Billie and Deana were summoned to the judge's chambers. They were to be there at two o'clock sharp or else. It seems that the chief told his father, the judge, about the formula and a decision was reached regarding Rocco's future. Elmer J. Fuddle's recipe was going back in business.

"Ladies," whispered the judge, "I have reached a decision about the infamous Rocco. He has had numerous run-ins with the law up north in the glorious state of Massachusetts. He's facing ten years on our chain gang for all the counts against him. Now if you two pretty ladies are as smart as you are beautiful, you will agree to the following terms for his release."

"Your Honor, we agree to everything, if you will let us get on our way," answered Deana.

"Now, young lady, don't be so quick to agree until you have heard the agreement."

"Yes, Your Honor, I can wait to hear your agreement. I mean judgment on the case."

"Well, now, that's more like it. The following are the terms for the release of Rocco the criminal," hollered the judge. The judge thought he was in the court room instead of his chambers, and his voice was higher than needed.

"First, you, Ms. Billie Joe, will supply me with the recipe for your grandpappy's moonshine."

"I can't do that!" cried Billie Joe. "I promised Grandpa that I would never give up the formula. I just won't agree to that condition Rocco will have to remain in jail. Theodore, you promised that you would not ask me to do that."

"Oh, did I? I wasn't sure. I was too intoxicated on your delicious and wonderful moonshine, my dear."

"Your Honor, you have to allow me to not break a promise to a grandparent," Billie Joe yelled.

"Well, young lady, I agree. We can't go around breaking our promises. Why if I allow that to happen, my son Theodore will be sending me to jail for what my Pa did in his moonshine days."

"Thank you, Your Honor. What are the rest of the requirements to release Rocco?"

"Well, I'm afraid that without the recipe, we won't be able to trust ya'll folks. So Rocco will have to be held in contempt of court and given community service at the restaurant, helping Maybell cook until you have paid the fine. One hundred bottles of moonshine each month for the next year."

"But, Your Honor, he only cooks Italian food," cried out Deana in an attempt to change things.

"Young lady, he will have to learn how to cook what we like here in the county," replied the judge.

"Yes, sir. He's very smart. He can learn new things. I'm sure," answered Billie Joe.

"Fine. Then it's a deal. You supply me, and he remains here until you have filled your quota."

"Yes, Your Honor. It's a deal."

"Officer, bring the prisoner in, please," whispered the grinning judge.

Within a few seconds, Rocco appeared. He looked very upset, ready to explode.

"What the hell is going on here?" he yelled. "I want a free lawyer. I have rights you know."

The judge wasn't too happy.

"Ya'll best calm down, young man, afore I throws ya back in jail. Your girlfriends have saved your ass form the chain gang. Even though I'm now having second thoughts about our deal. However, a deal is a deal, and I will stick to my word."

"Rock, be quiet," said Deana. "We have a good deal for you, but keep your temper under control."

"Yeah, Rock," added Billie Joe. "Keep your fucking mouth closed for once."

"Ya'll best listen to them, Rocco," advised the chief. "All right, all right, I get the message. Now let's hear this deal."

"Ya'll listen close, young man," answered the judge. "Here is the deal, and you don't have any choice because I am pronouncing sentence on you. Ya'll will be under my jurisdiction until I let you go. Do ya'll understand?"

"Yes, I, ya'll, understand." Rocco had to get one last shot at the judge.

"That does it," cried the judge. "Put this man in solitary for a week. We will see how much of a smart ass Yankee he is then."

"Rocco, we are all done with your stupid attitude!" yelled Billie Joe. "Your Honor, if you still want to go ahead with the deal, call us. Me and Deana are going home to Florida. We can complete everything by phone."

"Well, young ladies. I will give it some thought, but right now, it is looking pretty bad for your friend."

"Bye, Rock. I'll see you when you get home, whenever that is," said Billie Joe.

"Rock, call us and let me know how long you will be in jail on the chain gang," Deana whispered. "I'll tell Iris to get you a lawyer."

The judge interrupted her and said, "It's too late for a lawyer unless you want appeal his sentence. If that happens, I will keep him in solitary, and our deal will be dead for sure."

"Don't I have something to say about this?" asked Rocco.

All five of the people in the room looked at him, and in unison, they yelled, "No!" The judge turned to the officer and told him to take the prisoner away.

"You can't do this!" Rocco yelled as he went out the door.

"Young ladies, the deal is still in effect. I want to cool his heels for a while. I will offer him the deal next week. I'm sure he will come around and run with it."

"Thank you, Your Honor. I will start on the first shipment to you. Please give me an address to ship to."

"Billie, why don't we deliver the first one ourselves," replied Deana.

"Yes, that's a good idea, girls. We can have lunch together again," interrupted the chief.

******

Iris, Olga, and Pendleton listened to the Rocky horror story intently. Pendleton started laughing so hard he drooled on his new uniform jacket. "Bloody beautiful," he cried. "That dumb greaser belongs with the Mafia in jail."

"Now, Penny, you could be more forgiving for the poor soul. He will be in jail for a long time, I think," replied Iris.

"Yeah, my captain. He good man. Better than you. I think," answered Olga.

"Listen there's more," said Deana.

"That's right," Billie Joe added. "We can get him out of jail and home in six months. All I have to do is send moonshine to the judge. We have a deal."

"You are not using this bloody yacht for illegal activities," answered Pendleton.

"Well, Penny," said Deana, "until Rocco is out of jail, you are shut off."

"Bloody, what the hell, you can't threaten me with sex!" "I didn't threaten you with sex. I threatened you with no sex," replied Deana.

"And don't even think of me," added Billie Joe.

The captain glanced at Billie, then said, "You don't have the equipment I need."

"I'm built better than Deana," replied Billie Joe.

"I'm afraid not, young lady."

"That's enough, everyone," interrupted Iris. "We are going to do whatever we need to do to release Rocco." She looked at Olga. "Have you two forgotten how bad the food will be?"

"Very well," answered Pendleton. "I still hope he has to stay in jail for a long time."

Iris glanced around the room, then addressed the group. "All right then, it's agreed. We have to rescue Rocco from jail."

"I have a plan," replied Billie Joe. "We can deliver the first installment of moonshine to the judge in person, then grab Rocco on the way out of town and be across the border in a couple of hours."

"No, dear, that won't work. They will notify the Florida state police, and all of you will be in jail," answered Iris.

"I know what to do," interjected Deana. "We will get the judge in a compromising position with me. I have a special way of trapping men when I need help."

Iris looked at Pendleton as if to say, "Did she get you that way?" He looked back and smiled. He knew what Deana was talking about. It would be just like Admiral Hornblower. "That's a good idea!" he said to her.

"I like it," replied Billie Joe. "I can help by taking pictures with my cell phone and sending them back here right away so they can't be confiscated. The judge will have to let Rocco go. I'll tell him that I will send him some moonshine after we get home."

Olga had been quiet, but she wanted to be part of the rescue, so Rocco and her could keep having sex on a regular basis.

"Yeah, I go too. I can drive the getaway car," she said in an effort to be of some use.

"Yes, Olga, I'm sure we will need you in this operation," replied Billie Joe.

"Then it is settled," answered Iris. "We will go to Georgia and get him."

The captain wasn't sure it was such a good idea, but he didn't want to eat Olga's cooking ever again.

"Let's plan it like a precise military operation," he volunteered. "I will put a plan together. We can meet here tomorrow. I might even go with you."

"Very good," Iris volunteered. "Let's sleep on it. We will meet in the morning over tea."

******

In the morning, as Billie Joe served tea and crumpets, they chatted about the captain's plan. It was the popular agreement amongst the group that it was too detailed and would be hard to implement.

Deana suggested, "We shall just get him in bed and take pictures of him and me with my special equipment."

"Yes, that's the right thing to do," added Billie Joe. It will be quick and simple."

"What if he's gay?" asked Iris. "What then?"

"Then we get him in bed with Rocco," Deana answered.

"I'm going to get the first shipment of moonshine ready, so we can head out to get him," Billie Joe sang out as she got up to leave.

"What about my plan?" asked the captain.

"Yeah, not so good" answered Olga. She followed Billie Joe to the engine room to work on the first shipment.

Iris decided to help her brother. "Penny, it is a lovely plan. You just don't have the manpower to carry it out.

Deana felt bad for her honey and added, "Penny, why don't you direct things from here. Maybe you can find out if we can do this a legal way."

"No, I would just as soon let him rot in jail."

Episode 7

As the three girls drove to the town of Pigs Hollow in Georgia They chatted about Rocco as though he were deceased.

"I loved his cooking," said Deana.

"Yeah, like to get him sex," answered Olga. "He was good."

"Olga, all you think about is sex," Billie Joe countered. "I liked to have drinks with him. He was always getting into trouble and making our time exciting."

"Well, we can have him back soon. I'm dying to pull this one off," added Deana.

Just then a police car pulled up. It was Pearpecker again. His lights were flashing, and the siren was blasting. "Oh no, it's him again," said Deana.

"Ignore him. We have a judge in the pocket," answered Billie Joe.

"We better pull over. Olga, stop and see what the hell that rebel bastard wants. It's his fault that we are in all this mess," replied Deana.

"Yeah," she answered and almost ran at the cop of the road.

As they rolled down the window to talk to him, he appeared with his big head almost blocking out the sun.

"Do you ladies know who you're dealing with? I'm Officer Alutious P. Pearpecker of the Hogs Hollow Police Department."

"I thought you were with the Pigs Hollow Department," answered Deana.

"Well, what have we here? You look familiar, and so does this here vehicle."

"That's right, Officer," Billie sang out. "You have our friend Rocco in indentured servitude."

"Your friend is in what?" he asked.

"You know jail," she answered.

"Oh, you mean that tough mafia guy I had to straighten out with my Southern hospitality stick?"

"Yes, that's the one."

"Well, now ya'll, he is the reason I got fired by my pa, the chief of police, in Pigs Hollow. Did ya'll know that your friend is being held illegally. My pa said I shouldn't even have arrested him that day. They just kept him because the judge, my grandpa, wanted your recipe for moonshine."

"What?" yelled Billie. "They can't do that. Officer, ya'll want to get even with your pa? You can help us get Rocco back to Florida, and we will give you this shipment of moonshine instead of your grandpa, the judge."

"Ya'll caring contraband? I'm afraid I'll have to confiscate this shipment."

"You don't have to confiscate anything. Just help us get Rocco back."

"I don't think your friend wants to go home. I work for a different town, and ya'll are under arrest for smuggling moonshine into my town."

"Get lost," replied Billie. "If I don't give the judge this shipment, he will never let Rocco go."

"No matter," he said as he eyed José. "Now you have to get your three pretty selves out of
my jail. Ya'll better not let that pooch pee on me again."

Deana looked at Billie. "Let's give him some loving. Get your cameras ready."

"Yeah, I like him," replied Olga, as she got out of the car. The cop looked at her and smiled. He was smitten.

Billie Joe got out of the car and opened the trunk to get one of the bottles of moonshine which was in legitimate bottle marked with a famous scotch label.

"Here, Officer. Why don't you and Olga get to know each other and have a good time? We will pick her up right here tomorrow. You do make a pretty couple."

The cop lost track of what he was doing. He and Olga, holding hands, disappeared in the patrol car. They were both smiling.

"Let's go, Deana. I'll drive now. We have the right to take Rocco out of the state, and we will."

"That's right," answered Deana, "but let's not tell him. We can make him think that we rescued him, and he will owe us forever."

"You sure are a devious one," replied Billie Joe.

"Yes, I am," replied Deana. "Drive this blooming car over to Pigs Hollow, and we can get him right now. Does Olga carry a cell phone. We can't wait till tomorrow to retrieve her."

"Why, yes, she does. I have her number. Do you want to call her?"

"No, let her have some fun, then we will rescue her from fatso."

"I don't think she will want to be rescued. She seemed to like him."

"Well, she has to return with us," replied Deana.

"I hope so we need her for the tug of war. Let's get going. We can figure it out as we drive."

The Rolls entered town and stopped at the restaurant now sporting a new sign, which read Rocco's Homemade Pasta and Meatballs. Deana and Billie Joe entered to find him behind the counter. He had a chef's hat on his head was slightly cocked to show attitude.

"Hey, girls!" he yelled, a big smile came across his face. "Where have you been? I've been wondering about you two. Where is Olga?"

"Olga is on a date," answered Billie Joe, "keeping that fat rebel cop busy while we spring you."

"You can't spring me. I'll get arrested and have to serve my sentence in jail."

"Don't worry, Rock. Just give us some food while we check out the town and talk to the judge," replied Deana.

"Sure, what do you want to eat?" asked Rocco.

Billie Joe answered quickly, "Spaghetti and meat balls, of course."

"Coming right up," he said, then disappeared to the kitchen. While the two girls waited, the chief entered.

"Well, well, ladies, good to see ya'll again. Mind if I join you for lunch?"

"Ya'll can join us anytime, Chief," Billie Joe answered.

"What brings you back so soon?" he asked.

"We came to visit the prisoner Rocco."

"Oh yes, the mafia guy. Did you bring any moonshine?" he asked with a smile.

"Shore did. Would you like a bottle with lunch?" Billie Joe replied. She looked over to Deana and smiled, thereby sending the message that they would get the whole police department drunk, then simply drive away with Rocco in tow.

"Why, I certainly would," he replied.

"I'll be right back," Deana announced as she headed for the Rolls to retrieve a bottle of booze.

"Hurry back, dear," the chief called after her. "She's a real looker," he said to Billie Joe.

"What about me, Theodore? I thought ya'll liked Southern belles?"

"Oh I do, I really do, but she seems to have something special hidden under her clothing. There's a mystery. Something about her really appeals to me. I wonder what it is?"

"I don't know what that could be, Chief," Billie Joe replied, not having any idea about Deana's secret.

"Well, whatever it is, I would like to find out."

"I can talk to her, if you want."

Deana was back with the hooch. "Have a drink, Chief," she said.

Billie Joe smiled, then added, "Me too," with so much enthusiasm that the chief looked at her and smiled in a way that made one think he was picturing an afternoon delight.

Within one hour, they had the chief under the table, drunk as a skunk. They moved onto the judge and overcame him very quickly. He apparently was not much of a drinker. Two pretty girls, paying special attention, caused him to use bad judgment. Before he faded, they had him call in the last two grandsons.

The girls told them they needed a ride to see the town. Billie went with one, and Deana accompanied the other in two separate squad cars.

The next challenge was the restaurant and Rocco. The owner had three daughters, and Rocco had charmed them all into bed.

"Rocco," Deana asked, "why are you stalling around? We have to get to Florida before the judge and his family wake up. He is going to be pretty upset with us. If we don't get you this time, we won't be trusted enough to do it again."

Billie Joe was getting anxious also. "Rock," she whispered, "you have to come now. We still have to find Olga before we leave."

"I don't want to leave today. My friend is going out with me tonight."

"So tell your friend, whatever his name is, that you'll call him when we cross the Georgia line."

"It's a she, and I like her."

Deana stood and looked at him. "Rocco, are you telling me that you are in love? Why didn't you say that before we took the chance of going to jail?"

"I didn't know until she told me she liked me."

"Well," replied Billie Joe, "let's have a drink to celebrate. I'll get the moonshine out of the car."

"Don't bother. I have my vodka right here," he replied.

"I like the moonshine better," she said and went to the car. As she left, she gave Deana that look. They would get him drunk and hijack him.

"Rock, can I have a mixed drink?" asked Deana.

"Sure, I'll make it myself. What did you have in mind?"

"A vodka collins, please," replied Deana.

Billie Joe returned and sang out, "Don't bother. I have the good stuff. Use this instead of vodka."

"Rock?" she asked. "What is your girl friend's name?"

"Ricky," he answered.

"Ricky who?" Asked Deana.

"Her real name is Holly Rickenbacker."

"Pretty name," replied Billie Joe.

"Billie, I need your help," Deana asked.

"What's wrong, hon?" asked Billie Joe.

Deana's eyes were fixed on the window. They were moving from right to left following someone. Rocco was facing away from the window. He turned to see what she was looking at.

"Look, it's the judge, and he's shit faced. He can't even walk!" Rocco shouted.

"Be quiet. We got him drunk to get you out of here," Billie Joe answered.

"Jolly good," answered Rocco, now slurring his words slightly.

We got all of them drunk. That's why we have to get out of here before they wake up," replied Billie Joe.

"No, I'm staying. I am in love."

"What about Olga?" Asked Deana.

"She's screwing that fat hillbilly. So who cares about her?" Rocco replied.

"You have to come home with us. We need you on the boat. There is no one else as god as you in Key West. Let's go!" Billie Joe shouted.

"I'm not going to come hoooome," he answered, then passed out on the table.

"That stuff works fast." Deana smiled. "Let's get him in the car. Before he comes to, we have to be in Florida."

"You know we have to find a reason to stop him from coming back here to get his girlfriend. Why don't we tell him he got drunk because she told him she is pregnant?"

"Yes, blooming good," replied Deana. "She will piss off because he left without saying good-bye."

"Great idea. Let's get Olga. Call her and find out where to meet her."

******

The girls called and called, but Olga would not answer her phone. She apparently was enjoying her time with Officer Pearpecker. Unbeknownst to the girls, the two lovers were not very far away. Officer Pearpecker had taken her back to his old hunting grounds. He knew all the lovers' lane areas where his car wouldn't be spotted.

Rocco moaned and rolled over in the back seat. He was having a dream about sex. He moaned again, then started to call Deana's name followed by, "No, put it here. Oh, that's good."

Deana was embarrassed but Billie Joe was laughing.

"Billie, wake him up. I don't want him dreaming about me out loud like that."

"No, it sounds good to me. I hope he yells out some secrets about you two."

"There are no secrets between us. He tries, but I don't go, for it I don't think he could handle my special parts. If you know what I mean."

"Yeah, I know what you mean. Hey," shouted Billie Joe, "look at that cop car in the trees. I think that's Pearpecker and Olga. Let's have a look and see."

Deana whipped the Rolls over to the side of the road as fast as she could and made a U-turn to get back to the spot. As they walked up to the car, it was rocking and rolling. They weren't sure if they should get to close to it. He did after all have a gun and a bottle of moonshine inside the car. They could see one of Olga's nude size 12 feet sticking out the window. It was jiggling around to the beat of the old rock and roll song.

"Oh, Aleutian!" she screamed, "You are so talented. Yeah?"

"Ya'll aint seen anything yet, lovely lady. Watch this!" he yelled as the car rocked some more.

"Oh, Aleutian, you're the greatest!" Olga screamed.

Deana looked at Billie Joe and said, "We best not get to close."

"No, Deana, we have to get going before Rocco wakes up. My stuff is good, but it won't keep him out all day." She paused. "I don't think."

"Well, what do we do?" asked Deana."

Billie Joe was deep in thought and delayed her answer. "I don't know. Let's hit the car with a rock," she suggested.

Deana came back with, "Let's beep the horn in the Rolls."

"Okay, that should do it, and we can stay far enough away so we don't get shot."

They retired to the Rolls and started beeping. The first beep didn't have any effect, but on the second prolonged blast, two heads popped up. They both looked bewildered. The cop had his gun in his hand, and Olga had the bottle of booze in hers.

"What the blue blazes?" cried Pearpecker.

"Yeah," added Olga.

"Look," yelled Billie Joe, "we did it. They are up."

Deana wasn't too sure about the scene unfolding in front of them.

"I think we have a problem, Billie. The fat one is coming at us in his undies."

"He has his gun aimed at us too."

"You two crazy ladies get the hell out of that there vehicle now," he yelled as he aimed the gun at them. "Oh, it's you two," he said as he got closer.

"Billie, we are going to have a failure to communicate, I think," said Deana.

"You bet you are," the cop answered as he pulled his handcuffs out. "Step out of that vehicle, ya'll." "Deana, what should we do?" asked Billie Joe.

"You all ain't going to do nothing," answered Alutious. "I'm going to do the doing," he added, now stepping over near the bumper.

"What are you doing?" asked Deana.

The cop handcuffed them to the bumper of the Rolls and headed back to the police car. Olga was drunk, and the cop wasn't doing much better. They got right back to where they left off. The two of them were giggling and laughing loudly when another police car pulled up, looked at the Rolls, then stopped.

"Well, well, what do we have here?" one cop said to the other.

"It looks like some female prisoners are being detained by Officer Pearpecker to me," answered the other.

"We are not prisoners! We are civilians," answered Billie Joe.

"That's right, Officer, that blooming rapist has our friend captured in his car and won't let her go."

"What is your friend's name?" he asked.

"It's Olga," replied Deana.

"Olga? Ma'am you all wait here. I'll check with Officer Pearpecker. It looks to me like he has finally subdued her."

"How do you know that?" asked the younger officer.

"The car has stopped shaking," replied the senior officer.

"They were fooling around, and we have to go home," answered Billie Joe.

Just then, the radio in the second police car came on. The dispatcher said, "This is an all points bulletin. We want the white Rolls-Royce with three people in it to be brought to the judge's quarters in Pigs Hollow. That is, two pretty females and an ugly Italian Don Juan."

"Uh-oh," said Billie Joe. "We are in big trouble now."

"You sure are," yelled the first cop.

Officer Pearpecker jumped out of his car and saw the cops looking at him. He was stark naked. His belly hung over his groin and down to his genitals. He stopped in his tracks when he saw his superior looking at him.

"Pearpecker, what the hell are you doing? Are you raping that poor young thing in your automobile?"

"No, sir, she is my beloved girlfriend," he replied, then smiled.

"Pearpecker, get dressed and tell her to get dressed. What the hell are these two young ladies doing handcuffed to their car?"

"They were interfering in my lovemaking, sir."

"What! Are you insane? Do you want to get us sued to kingdom come?"

Billie Joe couldn't resist. "Hey, fatso, let us go, or we'll sue all of you. We want our friend Olga back also."

"Don't worry, ma'am. Everything will be all right," replied the boss.

He then looked at Pearpecker. "Aleutian," he yelled, "get your ass in gear. Release these girls and get back to work. We'll talk later."

Deana was getting upset and let the head guy know it.

"Officer," she cried, "you release us right now, or I'll call my mother. She is the head of the British Secret Service."

"Yes, ma'am, you don't have to threaten me with the red coats. We already kicked their ass once. Didn't we?"

Just then, there was a loud moan from the backseat of the Rolls.

"You shitheads are dead as far as I'm concerned," yelled Rocco. He was halfway out the door, still drunk, and as always, ready for a fight.

"Who the hell are you?" cried the boss.

"He's the mafia," yelled Pearpecker.

Rocco, not knowing what had transpired, his shirt ripped and showing his very hairy chest, looked extremely menacing.

"There's no such thing as the mafia. You friggin' hillbillies," he returned, then started to advance toward the cops.

"Look out!" hollered Pearpecker. "He's crazy. I've dealt with him before. I had to use my stick on him. I think he is an escapee from Pigs Hollow."

Rocco tore into the hillbilly cop with vengeance and malice.

"You overgrown tub of shit mixed with cat fish. I would have kicked your fat ass, if you didn't have that overgrown night stick."

The head cop was showing alarm now at the thought of Rocco beating up his officer. Rocco was still staggering toward him and cursing out loud.

"I'll kick your Southern ass," he screamed, then started running at Pearpecker. Pearpecker was full dressed now and decided to stop Rocco. He raised his stick, ready to strike when all of a sudden, Rocco went down like a bag of sand on the edge of an overflowing river. He was screaming and writhing.

"Ya'll being a little too frightening," said the boss cop as he hit the button on the Taser again. Rocco jerked, then lay still. "We had better get to the bottom of this here mess, Pearpecker."

"Listen, Officer," said Billie Joe in her best Southern drawl. "We won't cause any legal trouble if you let us all go back to Florida."

"Ma'am I have to get to the bottom of this mess. Then, we will see about where you people are going. Now, Pearpecker, what the hell is going on here boy?"

"Well, boss, the mafia guy was falsely arrested by the judge, my granpa.

The girls interrupted my lovemaking with my darling, Olga, so I slowed them down for a while by cuffing them. Olga here is my soul mate."

The boss cop looked at Pearpecker and scratched his head.

"You the dumbest son of a bitch I ever did know, Pearpecker. No wonder your pa got rid of you over at Pigs Hollow. You girls take this here mafia man and get the hell out of the county and the state. First, promise that you won't cause any legal problems for my department."

"Yes, sir," replied Billie Joe, "we promise."

"Well then, all of you, scat!" answered the cop.

"Boss, what about the all points bulletin?" asked Pearpecker.

"Pearpecker, we have before us a chance to avoid a lawsuit that would end with you in prison for rape. Don't you want to remain free?"

"Why, of course I do, boss."

"Then, let it go." He turned to the group, looked Rocco over, then thought awhile. "Well, folks, be on your way and don't come back here soon, please."

******

Back aboard the ship, Iris and Pendleton were concerned about the girls. It had been three days since they went for Rocco.

"Iris, where do you think they are right now?" asked Pendleton.

"I'm not sure they should be in Florida by now. I hope we hear from them soon. I'm getting worried about this whole situation."

"Yes, I'm worried about the girls also, but Rocco deserves anything he gets."

"Now, Penny, give him some rope. He will be great by the time we get him retrained."

"I would like it better if he were gone altogether."

******

The Rolls Royce was entering the town of Branson Florida when Rocco decided he had to stop for a drink at the local watering hole. Billie Joe was driving and didn't want to stop.

"Billie Joe, stop now or else," threatened Rocco.

Deana didn't like his tone and let him know it.

"Rocco," she said, "you can't talk to us that way. We just saved your ass from jail. You owe us big time, mate."

"All right then, please stop. I need a drink to make this headache go away."

Deana looked at Billie Joe and asked her to pull over for a couple of hours. Billie Joe glanced in the rear-view mirror. "Rock, you had better not get us in any more trouble."

Olga suddenly became interested. She loved drinking with Rocco. "I go to help," she said as the car stopped.

"We might as well all go in. Consider this the last pit stop between her and Key West," replied Deana.

"Who died and left you in charge?" answered Rocco.

Deana smiled at him and said, "Iris. It's her money we're spending."

"Let's just go in and get this over with," replied Billie Joe.

"Look at the marquee," she yelled. "Eddie Money is here. He's my favorite country singer."

"He stinks," replied Rocco."

"Yeah, I like Money," answered Olga.

The inside of the lounge was in better condition than the exterior. The owner hadn't repaired outside after the last hurricane. The four of them found a table near the stage and settled down for drinks and some good old-fashioned entertainment. A waitress took their drink order and left some popcorn on the table. The table behind was surrounded with local workers looking for some fun and entertainment also. It didn't take long for one of them to bump Rocco's chair. The second time it happened, Rocco turned around and gave the guy the eye.

"Stop hitting my chair, you stupid rebel," Rocco yelled.

"Hey, Yankee snow bird, blow it out your hole," he yelled back. Billie and Deana were not in the mood for another jail run.

"That's it, Rock. We are leaving," Deana said. "Are you coming or not?"

"You can't go anywhere. I have the keys," Rocco yelled back.

Just then, the man behind them punched Rocco in the back of the head.

Olga reacted by toppling over the table and spilling all the drinks on the
floor. Billie Joe and Deana ran for the door and out to the car. When the man hit Rocco, the car keys went flying up in the air, and Billie Joe caught them.

"Let's give them a minute to get out here, then we are leaving," cried Deana.

"That's fine with me," answered Billie Joe. "I hear a police car coming."

Inside the bar, the war had just started. Rocco and Olga were cleaning house. They finally came running out.

"Quick, let's get out of here," yelled Rocco.

"Me too," hollered Olga.

"Hit it," Billie Joe yelled to Deana.

The big Rolls left rubber and sped off toward the yacht.

Episode 8

They arrived at the boat, and Iris and Pendleton were happy to see them because with both the cooks gone, they had to eat out every night.

It was Rocco birthday. They know Rocco likes cannolis, so they have a party on the upper deck.

He never had a birthday party from his friends.

"This is great," he yelled "Where are my gifts?"

"Here," replied Iris, as she handed him some cannolis.

Pendleton gave Rocco a gift also. It's a cookbook called *Stew Aid for the Chef*, accompanied by a chef's hat, saying, "The Greatest Cook in Florida."

"Pendleton, what's this *Stew Aid* crap?"

"It's for cooks. The guy at the store said you sounded like that to him."

Deana and Billie Joe were still upset with him and won't give him a gift.

Olga gave him a big kiss. "Rock," she whispered in his ear, "I will be waiting for you in my room with your big present later."

Iris interrupted with her announcement, "Folks, after this party, I want everyone to stay here. We will take this time to have a meeting."

Iris has a hot love connection, looking toward Nicole for completion.

She brought up the thought of staying in Key West, instead of returning to New York City the following season.

"We are becoming Conks in the Conk republic," Iris told them. If we stay, I cannot pay you for the summer."

Billie was happy she had a great brewing business and had all the kids getting beer bottles for her. She was making her private labels with Pendleton's laptop and printer. Rocco has cooking business going. He liked the warm weather.

Olga liked the warm weather and all the activity. She wanted to stay near Tyler. Deana is happy anywhere she can dress up pretty.

Pendleton was upset. He wanted to be with his cronies in New York.

"Well," Iris says, "we have one against and the rest for. We will stay."

"I don't want to stay," Pendleton cried out.

"Yippy," Rocco yelled, "I can make money."

"Okay. Folks, let's calm down. We have two weeks of bookings to take care of. We do have to make money to stay in business. Don't we? Deana has a booking with a prominent family from Connecticut consisting of five people. A mom, dad, and son, and daughter-in-law, with their fourteen-year0old daughter. They will arrive tomorrow. Billie, get as much money as you can out of these guest. Rocco, pick them up at the airport in the Rolls." She stopped talking for a second. "Deana and Rocco, get some more catering going."

The next day, Deana gave her stateroom to honeymoon couple, mom and dad. She will bunk with Iris until they leave. That night, at bedtime, Deana and Iris are getting ready to sleep in the same bed.

"Deana, you're beautiful. I can see why Penny has such interest in you."

"Thank you, Iris. Penny and I have a special relationship, but we will never get married."

"Why not? He is a good man. He will always be there for you," replied Iris.

"I can't get into that right now, but let's just say I have to wait for the right laws to be introduced."

"Deana, tomorrow you can use the Rolls to do the shopping and riding them around Key West. Make sure you put the flowers on the table."

"What do you mean, Iris?"

"Make sure they are getting the watered liquor," Iris told her.

The next day, Iris tells Penny to babysit the kid. "Show her how to waterski," Iris said.

Penny doesn't know how to do any sports, so he handed her over to Billie Joe. "I'm the captain," he squealed. "It's not my job to babysit."

Billie Joe handed her back and replied, "You're the captain of nothing. You're a deckhand now. Iris is the captain. It's so good to have a pretty

woman for a leader. Isn't it, Penny?"

The kid just looked at them. Penny walked away, mumbling under his breath about Iris. Billie Joe then took the kid back to help with her duties. "What's your name, honey?"

"I'm Mary J. Murray Ferrara," she answered.

"Well, Mary J., would you like to help me do my work? It will give you something to do for a while, and you can learn your way around the ship.

"All right. Are there any boys around here? I'm horny. Do you mind if I smoke?"

"Let's just start filling these beer bottles. I'll see if I can find some boys for you. No, you can't smoke on board the yacht. It's too dangerous, and you're too young."

"I'm not young. I'm fourteen, and I know more about life than you did when you were twenty-one."

"Okay, then let's go. I'll drop you off at the mall."

Within ten minutes, Mary had met a bar owner's son named Derek. He bought her a goody, so she invited him aboard the boat.

Billie Joe picked them up at the mall, brought them home, and put them both to work bottling some beer. She went to get more supplies.

"Look," said José, "these two are getting drunk. They are drinking more than they are bottling."

"Yeah," replied Robin, "we have to stop them before they overdose."

"You don't overdose on beer, dummy." Batman laughed. "You get drunk and throw up."

"He's right," added Maxi. "We have to stop them. They are much too young. The captain can go to jail if they get caught."

The cat looked up and answered Maxi, "Not good. We will be homeless. Even though I condone their behavior, we must stop them now."

"I'll pull the fire alarm station," answered Robin.

"You can't reach it," replied Batman.

"All right, boys and girls. Calm down. I have a much more civilized way to stop them," added Maxi. "I'm going to do a fly-over and poop on them."

"Oh boy, I want to watch," replied José.

"Here goes," answered Maxi as he took off. "Bombs away," he squawked as he circled over their heads.

"Wow," said the cat, "a direct hit. He's good."

Robin was excited. "Yeah, what a shot. We will have to buy Maxi a drink."

"Yes," answered José. "Look the boy is wiping the poop stuff of his face. He was looking up.

Now the girl is wiping her head. Maxi got her too."

"Watch out, Maxi. The boy has something in his hand. He might throw it at you," warned Batman.

"I'll get him," answered the cat as he leapt on the boy's shoulder with his claws out.

José started barking then ran to the girl and peed on her foot. She looked at him in disgust.

"You filthy mutt," she yelled, then ran out of the room. The boy followed.

"Yippy," cried Maxi as he came sweeping in to land.

"You did it," answered the cat.

"We did it!" cried José. Billie Joe returned to check on the kids. She was amazed at this scene. She saw all the animals, screamed at the sight of the two mice, then jumped on the chair.

"What are you doing with these rats?" she asked José. "Kill them before they get me!" José knew he couldn't answer her so he ran over, jumped on the chair and rubbed against her leg. The rest of the gang quietly left the room. José caught up with them in the kitchen.

"Who the hell does she think she is," asked Batman, "calling us rats? That is like calling a whale a fish."

"I'm sorry, guys, but she is a very nice lady. I'm sure she didn't mean to hurt your feelings," answered José.

"Well, at least, we saved our home," squawked Maxi. "What the heck is Coco doing over there?"

"It looks like she is slurping up the spilled beer. I hope she doesn't get any poop with it," said Robin.

"Don't worry," answered José. "She wouldn't know the difference. She will eat anything when she is drunk. I once watched her eat a dirty stocking. She was legless! We really have to try harder to get her to Alcoholics Anonymous. One of these days, she is going to poison herself."

******

One week later, Iris and the crew were meeting again to keep the guests busy. Iris was, as usual, in charge of things with Penny pouting and complaining.

"Iris," said the captain, "I don't understand why I have to babysit that kid. She is old enough to take care of herself."

"Penny, dear brother, she was caught in the engine room smoking and drinking the moonshine. Do you want to lose the yacht to a fire or some other legal thing?"

"Well, we could chain her in the forward locker, couldn't we?"

"I suppose that would be a great idea, but her parents would come looking for her sooner or later."

"Iris, she is a real hellion. I can't keep up with her. From now on, no more kids on the boat."

"Oh, Penny, you men are all useless," replied Billie Joe. "I'll take her off your hands if you let me use your computer to make more labels for my beer bottles."

"That's a deal, young lady. I'll even supply the paper."

"Let's get on with the meeting," said Iris. "Rocco, what's the latest on Olga's training for the tug of war."

"She is in great shape except for the hair on her back. It grows all the way down to her armpits and keeps getting caught in the tug rope. When this happens, it hurts, so she releases her grip and falls down."

"My god!" yelled Penny. "She sounds terrific to me. I must see her back as soon as I can. Rocco, I'll give you some money if you arrange it."

"Listen, Captain, she isn't too excited about you ever since you stole her Marilyn doll."

"But she beat me up. We are even, aren't we?"

"I'll ask her, but she doesn't like to have people gawking at her. You will have to be sneaky. How much are you going to pay me?"

"Gentlemen, stop talking about Olga like she is a freak. I forbid you to look at her, Penny. Rocco just get her in shape, so she will win the tug."

"I was thinking that she could pull against the boat when it is running and in gear. What do ya think, Captain?"

"Hell no, she's liable to break something."

"This meeting is over, folks, except one thing. Deana, how are our guests doing? Other than the girl, that is."

"We are keeping them busy. They seem to be having fun. I think the son-in-law is gay he seems to prefer the gay bars."

"Well," replied Iris, "let's take them to Feathers. We can leave in about one hour. Anyone else care to join us?"

Rocco jumped up to leave, but on the way out of the cabin, he said, "I wouldn't be caught dead in there again even though that Nicole chick digs me."

"Rock, you flatter yourself." Penny giggled. "She is gay, you bloody dumb bastard."

"Who are you calling dumb? I can teach you a thing or two about women."

"Very well, I will take you up on that promise. We will have a contest to see who can get the most women between now and Christmas."

"That's fine with me. Let's bet on it. If I win, you pay me one hundred dollars. If you win, I will get Olga to let you touch her back hair."

"Not so fast, you blooming mafia enforcer. I want to touch her hairy legs also."

"I don't think that will work. She is going to shave them for the tug of war."

"Well, what about her armpits?"

"Sure, it's a deal. We start right now."

Iris had had enough. "Rocco, I want you to drive us to feathers in the Rolls-Royce now, please."

The bunch of them piled into the Rolls and headed for Nicole's nightclub. When they got there, Rocco elected to stay in the car. The rest, including the captain, went inside.

Rock made a phone call to Olga to meet him at the bar across the street from Feathers. Olga showed up about one half hour later. "Rock, you want me to help you drink?"

"Yeah, all the fools are in the gay bar over there. I won't pay the high prices for their crazy drinks."

"Not me either," replied Olga.

Meanwhile, in Feathers, the guests and the rest of the crew were getting loaded. "Penny, let's go in the bathroom for a romp."

"Deana, behave yourself," replied Iris. "I want to get Nicole in there first."

"Penny, come on. We will use it first."

"Deana, darling, I like some privacy. Why don't we find a room?"

"Where's your sense of adventure, Penny dearest?"

"I don't have one."

Deana looked at Iris. "It's all yours. Have fun."

Meanwhile, back at the other bar, Rocco and Olga were getting smashed.

His driving skills were definitely impaired by now, and Olga wasn't doing much better.

"Olga, let's go home and make out," Rock said, his grin was from ear to ear.

"Yeah, we make love all day, for long time. You think I am hot girl?"

"Sure, you're hot. Let's go."

Put a slot about the animals betting on Olga. They placed all their valuable bones and things in the pot. The other owners heard about Olga's special training and hired the wringer, Ernie Liftland.

She pulled out the cleat, and it hit someone important. Artie Liftland was on Olympic team but got cut. Billie Joe found out about the wringer and tried to swoop him and would sabotage him for the tug of war. George, the police chief, came to them for more booze and said Ernie was criminal and got him arrested for a while to get him out of the contest. The four bars put the best men in the tug. Tyler was main man for Rose's Calico Kitchen, and they sent their best. The Indian bar sent BaBa Alie. The tug was to be judged by Bo Bo Brazil. Guest were delighted and thought Olga would have championship tug of war. Rocco was the only one to get Olga going. She was basically lazy.

Billie was spotting Olga in her weight lifting so Rocco gets his work done. She edged her on to get the man in her life, Tyler, the bronze hero.

Each crew went. Iris can't believe how dumb they are. They drank watered-down drinks.

Deana and Billie Joe knew Iris took over the boat. Deana wanted her half-partnership and told Iris. Iris gave her a small interest in the boat. Iris talked about the tug of war, pushed the girls to win, and helped Olga be in shape. Olga was constantly lifting weights and working out. All the bar owners were asking to extend the tug. They have a meeting at Feathers chaired by Nicole.

Nicole talked to Iris. "We can drag this out to sell more drinks."

They have to convince the other owners to do the same. They put on a show in each bar to get their name going. Olga didn't get it. She was confused about the fun part of it because of the language barrier and knocks out BaBa Alie for touching her. The bar owner was pissed off about Olga. Iris talked to him to smooth it out. Later, he came to her boat with other owners to have drinks. Iris was so sexy, she turned on all the owners. Nicole got pissed.

Billie Joe said, "Iris is acting like a ho."

Deana said, "It's wrong to talk that way. Iris wants to have a fund to help each other out through hard times, summer storms."

The owners all wanted Rocco to work for them tomorrow, but Iris wanted a cut of the top. They have to pay her. The next meeting would be at Rose's Knockout. A magazine writer from Pendleton's past Rex Ashley wanted to do article on chartering B&B. They met with him at Rose's bar. Using borrowed chairs, they had an extravaganza dance to sway the writer. Each owner was trying to get him to favor their boat. It's a dress-up occasion. Rocco catered the affair, and Iris collected the money. A few of them tried not to pay, but Iris was ahead of them. She told them if they don't pay, Olga and Rocco would collect it for her. The owners that couldn't pay can trade goods such as crabs. If they don't pay, they don't get Rocco to cook.

Iris knew what the writer liked and got Rocco to cook for him to slant his writing in Iris's way. The writer was showing pictures on bulletin board to show his progress and how he was ratting them. He told them he would let them know who was favored amongst them in next month's mag. He went with Iris for a nightcap and some other favors. Her boat became the winner. The bar owners had a meeting to make her the honorary Conk princess for helping them find their way. Nicole gave her a kiss and put some emotion into it, but to others, it looked innocent.

After the tug, all the bars had a good take and decided to pool their money to protect them from hurricane season. Iris and the gang were new to the hurricane problems. Iris came up with idea to discuss with the five owners who own bars and charter boats. When season came they will run a gala then have a party. The guest would go from ship to ship to try each chef. The boats were rafted up off and island. Iris showed the others how to make money with tricks. Each boat would host each other's guest at the dock or the beach or nearby island. They all wind up at Booties for big dance, and the captains thanked their guests. Iris had Deana and Billie Joe teach the captains how to dance for the party. They have to clean up their act. They were restarting a forty-year tradition on the island called Taste of the Bounty.

Episode 9

Iris got news about four librarians coming to boat. She and Deana talked about how to handle them. Iris was happy about delaying the tug. This worked out good for them to get some extra money.

She told Deana, "Take them shopping, then we'll take them dancing."

Iris took them out to dance with Deana and Billie. They all got feeling good. One of the librarians liked Penny who was dressed up as girl and looked very nice. Iris told him he has to help out by dancing with her. Penny didn't like it. But he helped out. The other girls didn't know their friend was gay. Deana was dancing with one of the gay guys. He wanted her bra. Iris and Nicole danced together, and they were rubbing and feeling hot about it. Olga came to the bar and told them someone was trying to hurt José. They got back to the ship and caught BaBa Alie. They had a meeting with other bar owners about punishment. The others decided to make him help Rocco paint for a week.

Rock told him if he helped Olga win, he won't have to work. Rock would cover for him. Rocco was helping Olga with tug. He painted a pair of latex gloves to match her skin, and Luke sent a special glue to hold on to the rope. If Olga wins, he would put the tug rope in the truck, so no one will find out about the gloves. They would have a party on boat and hire a piano player. He was good and liked to think he was Geno Biennially. His name was Tony Guilloche.

Next morning, Rocco made them breakfast and gave Tina, one of the librarians, extra juice. He liked Tina. The lesbian named Kimberly was talking with Tina, and Tina said, "You hit it off with, what's her name, Penny?"

They asked Deana what is in store for the day, and Andy came by. All the girls were drooling over him. Deana told Andy she will pay him to take them to the shops in the Rolls, especially the shop Iris owns. Andy and Tina went to the bar to do research. He has a room at the hotel, and he and Tina had sex. The other librarians didn't fall for Andy's research trick. They asked where the books were.

Phyllis liked Andy also and asked how he was. Nicole had them to her bar for a buffet. They all went to Feathers in the Rolls and started drinking. Andy was the driver. They had a madrigal's party. To get certain color beads, they had to show their breasts. The librarians talked Phyllis into lift her blouse. She went too fast. Andy caught enough to get excited. They had karaoke, and they sounded good. Rocco found out where they were and went there to get Tina. Or whoever he could get.

All the girls liked the young Andy, and Rocco got nothing. Phyllis invited Rocco to her cabin. He went there to find Phyllis and went in the lesbian room by accident. She was happy to see a man and gave him a quickie. Iris called Deana on the cell to come back to the boat. She wanted a meeting because Alie has been arrested as terrorist. At the boat, they learned why Alie was picked up. Iris told them the other bars were trying to get him out. Rocco wanted to know why Alie is in jail.

Rocco wanted the one who squealed on him because something smelled bad. "People are going to think it's us."

Rocco did his own investigation and found an outsider who wanted a lot of winnings from the tug. Rocco and Olga found him and worked him over, so Alie won't get in trouble with the law for retaliation. His name was Tommy Calivaa, gay guy who couldn't make it with Alie. Rocco told all the others to bar him and all the betters not to bet with him.

Alie now owed her and Rocco a debt of honor.

Iris wanted to meet with Nicole to have tea and talk. Deana and Billie giggled. Billie said "Kissy, kissy me" as Iris left. Nicole could cover the bets if nothing happened. They could win thirty-five thousand. Nicole said she had to close the books soon. Alie's sister came to visit him. She's a doctor and would stay for a week. In six months, he came to California to live there. She found out about rope pull and thought it the latest thing. He explained to her that a lot of people were depending on him to win some money for their families. He had a discussion with his sister, and he wanted to stay in Key West. He called Iris to talk to the sister about him staying

The final date was set for the rope pull at the latest meeting. One owner wanted it on Friday. Nicole suggested Saturday so no one has to go to work Sunday morning. They decided to have five rope pulls. Each owner would sponsor a pull to make as much money for their bar as they can. Rocco got his glove glue ready for Olga. He had no idea how strong she is.

Olga asked him why they need the glue. She told him when she worked at the docks in Russia, she always used bare hands to pull in the ships, even in the winter.

Daniel Murphy was chosen to be first at the glistening clover to go against local cops. He would supply iced tea all night for five dollars but raise the beer prices all night. They all agreed to do the same each time it's their turn so they can make money.

Episode 10

Nicole said to Iris, "I need to talk to you about selling my bar, Booties, in New York City. I want you to watch my place here while I'm gone. I want you to keep Rocco and Penny away from the bar. Keep Rocco away from the girls."

Iris asked when she will be back. Nicole told Iris she has her life savings into the bar. Iris wanted to go and help Nicole with negations. The bond between them was getting closer. Nicole was alone in new York and was meeting with Maggie Hogan who wanted to turn it into an ale's bar. Nicole wanted it to stay the same. Maggie wanted Nicole to hold paper. Nicole wanted 130 up front and 250 for the restaurant. Maggie wanted the whole thing and needed money. She could pay 380 in cash.

Nicole told Iris she had a buyer and needed another week to close the deal. Iris told her that Rocco did something to the girls. Nicole told the buyer she will hold paper to close the deal. She knew that lesbian bars didn't seem to make it. She had to go back to Feathers, and the closing will be in a couple of weeks.

Rocco wanted to rent Feathers to cook up a big meal for his friends. They were having a reunion. He would charge twenty dollars per head. She will get five plus the bar. Nicole told Rocco in Italian that if any trouble broke out, she would cut of his balls and stuff them up his ass. Rocco wanted to know where she learned Italian. Iris told Nicole not to close the bar to Rocco. Nicole should open the bar for her customers and Rocco friends. Rock's party was scheduled. Iris and Nicole knew this was important to Rock and made it look good in front of his friends. The next staff meeting brought up a discussion about Rock being a pain in the ass. Nicole received an offer more than Meg Hogan was offering. She told Meg cash only, then sold it to M&M company.

Maggie wasn't happy. Maggie caused trouble in Florida. Nicole kicked ass. Iris was happy Nicole was coming back. Iris had Rocco fixing things up at Feathers, so the tug will be just right. Waiting for Nicole was long. The weather was bad. It had been raining for three days. They all had Billie's beer, and the bunch of them got drunk. They all went to Rose's Knockout to have a corned beef sandwich, the best on the island.

Rocco told Harry to make a better sandwich. Harry replied to Rocco, "At least my food makes money." Rocco wanted to argue about cooking, but Iris wanted to leave before trouble started. Harry threw a fish at Rocco. Rocco tried to stop it, and his wig fell off. Harry sucker-punched Rock. The girls jumped in to save Rock. Rocco called Harry a cheap Irish bastard even though he was Swedish. Rocco was pissed because he lost. Iris was mad. It was still raining. Deana wanted to raid Penny's closets. They found some clothing that belonged to one of the librarians. Iris said they better check their own clothing, especially undies.

They went back to the saloon to sort the CDs out. They asked Billie to help and find out Billie Joe has a nice voice. They all began to dance to the music and talked about men. They called them names, except for Andres. They like his extra large penis. They had a PJ party until the rain stopped.

Iris got in the Rolls to go downtown and found tarps in the backseat and in the trunk. Iris was furious and wanted to kill Rocco. "Just can't believe that Rocco is such an idiot." The girls got Rocco.

He said, "They're just tarps." They showed him the scratch in the door, and he said, "We can fix it."

This ruined the shopping trip. Iris wanted to kill Rocco. Andres fixed the scratch with coat of arms. Iris liked it and got Andy to come back to bed with her. Rocco and Galotch were discussing a party the next morning at breakfast in the Calico Kitchen. He told Rocco it's for charity, for the bag people of the island. He won't make money for himself. Rocco agreed to do it for charity. They went to Knights'

Hall and tried to get the ballroom free. Rocco suggested the boat, but they got the hall cheap. Rocco and Andy borrowed a boat and got stuck, and the Coast Guard helped. Rocco thought all the money from the ball was going to charity, but Galotch was selling his CDs to make a profit. They sold the tickets for eight dollars to the public but five to sail boaters who were considered cheap bastards. Rocco put something in the sail boaters' food to give them the shits.

Billie Joe brought the food to the boaters' table so Rocco won't get blamed. The sail boaters all got the shits the next day. Rocco said he was capable of giving them the shits with either hand. "I'm extra dangerous," he said.

Billie said, "What did you say?" He repeated it. She told him he's ambidextrous. The door prize was one of Galotch's CDs, instead of a television. No one cares except Rocco. They had a raffle winner, got a couple bottles of booze, homemade vodka. Olga threatened them with painful death if they didn't buy raffle. End day, money was counted, and they saw that Galotch was cheating.

He told Rocco about the expenses. "CDs cost money," he said.

But Rocco knew he was lying because of the television. Rocco told Iris to take care of Galotch. The next day, Olga and Rocco tied him to the deck and allowed him to get sunburned. Iris saw this and allowed it to go on, figuring they have a good reason. Iris wanted Rocco to stop playing games and get Olga trained for the pull.

Episode 11

The first rope pull was on the beach at Harry's Knockout bar. Iris and the gang went to the event. Deana babysat Rocco because of Harry. At the bar, they had the a buffet. They announced that the two teams were the best firemen and cops in the Key West. Harry said, "May the best team win," and he announced Bo Bo Brazil was the judge.

Penny's group was watching to see who was the best to prepare for their turn. Each event bar would charge an admission fee to go to charity. Billie was collecting bottles. Harry thought it's nice of Billie Joe to clean off the tables. Billie Joe was stealing the bottles. Whoever won this event would compete against the Calico Kitchen. The Glistening Clover wants to be next as was preplanned and was arguing with Iris. It was announced that a change was needed from the Kitchen to the Clover being next The next rope pull will be at the Glistening Clover at night, no buffet, half price on drinks instead in the form of happy hour. The cops lost to the firemen, so the firemen would pull against the Glistening Clover. The cook's name is Peggy Fortain, ex-roller derby queen, tough as nails. Murphy's son Patrick was geek leader and well built. The bouncer Danny Shea, the handy man Timmy Parker, and his waitress sister Debby Parker were the team for the Glistening Clover.

The event would be on Friday night, then happy hour. Coast Guard men just wanted to drink their share. Billie Joe was happy to sell her beer for happy hour at the Glistening Clover tug. The event happened, and the firemen lost. Everyone but the firemen were happy, and they praised Billie's beer. Raining again, they started karaoke, and everyone was singing. Someone spotted a water spout, and it caved in the roof of the Glistening Clover, breaking one of Peggy's arms, but the party went on.

They announced that the next round would be between the Calico Kitchen and the Glistening Clover at the Calico Kitchen. They will have big fish buffet put on before the event. The Glistening Clovers were to compete against the Calico Kitchen. The Glistening Clover has to scurry to replace Peggy. Because of the rules, they had to replace teammates with the same gender. Or no replacement at all.

During the week, the Glistening Clover was closed by the health department for the damage. Daniel Murphy asked Iris for an extension and Rocco for a loan because he had no insurance to repair the roof. He was busy and needed to find another person for the tug of war. They did the pull and won with four people. BaBa Alie got out of jail just in time and gave them encouragement. Daniel Murphy won enough to repair the roof of the bar. The Calico Kitchen lost. Harry's Knockout wanted to hire BaBa to be on their team. Iris wanted him too.

Episode 12

Nicole's cousin sushi chef Goushu, a jazz artist and a shrimp boat operator, liked cooking and wanted to be a jazz singer. Iris fired her pianist. Goushu was singing while waiting for something, and Iris heard him. Iris invited him to sing on board. She said, "We can make a singer on the boat out of him." Iris asked him to do a one-night performance to sing on the boat. They had a private gathering, and he told them he was getting up a trio.

Iris needed him and his group on boat. He had vacation and said yes. They gave him a room for the night. He was well-liked, good-looking, and about twenty-eight years old. Next morning, he saw Rocco trying to catch fish, and he helped Rocco catch more fish. Rock liked him, and they were like birds of the same feather. He told Rocco he was a chef and Rocco and him could cook together. Goushu told Rocco how to make the meals look good and told Rocco to call him Be Be. He sounded like Victor Moan's great voice. Iris tried to steal him away from his boss. Be Be liked to dance and has a great personality. He was a good influence on Rocco. The whole group liked him. He had a problem with English, causing some confusion, except when Nicole was around to translate for him. He's teaching Rocco Japanese and told Rocco, "No tami tami on the matt."

Rocco learned a little of his language and swore in Japanese, English, and Italian. Be Be went back to Nicole and said, "When I come back, I show you how to make shamoe shamoe."

At the club Feathers, he was talking to Nicole. She told him he did a good job as a chef and shouldn't leave it, but if he wanted, he will be her chef. Nicole was going to build a kitchen. It's going to be Italian Japanese restaurant. She wanted Goushu to manage it and teach Rocco how to cook. She couldn't pay what he was worth but will make him a partner. He could sing three nights a week, and Rocco would be back-up cook. Goushu agreed and they set up a meeting with Rocco. Rocco and Iris met them at Feathers at eight o'clock, and Nicole told Iris about deal with Goushu.

Iris said she will back it up. "We can be just like one of the big stores and cover the whole island."

At a table in the back office, they told Rocco he was family and they wanted him to cook in the new Japanese Italian restaurant. He would be the head chef, but he needed to be able to cook Japanese. Also, Goushu would be singing jazz, and he would be the head of the Japanese department. Rocco was extremely happy and agreed to learn from Goushu, and he would teach him Italian cuisine. "I'll do all the painting and fixing up," he said. Rocco came up with a deal that will make him a partner. He asked for such a small amount that Iris could give him a little more and added conditions.

Rocco said he was still the poorest man in the world but happy. Goushu was leaving his job. But the boss talked him into staying with a big raise. Goushu wanted to do it, but he wanted to have his jazz career. Rocco got the news to Olga about the deal. She would be doing the prep work, and she would be the handyman at the new restaurant. She was happy to have a title of prep chef. Rocco would teach her how to be good American cook. She would get more pay as cook's helper, and she would be a bouncer at night. Iris found out about offer to Goushu from his boss and countered it. She would help him put his jazz band together by talking to a big shot in the music industry. She would help him put out a CD. Iris made him sign a contract for five years.

He said, "Yes, but I have to have a queen's night each week."

She agreed, and they signed the contract. Iris said, "The bigger the crowd, the more money. We need to attract the gay crowd."

They had a signing party and celebrated at Calico Kitchen to entice Ba Ba Alie to be on their tug team—two owners, wife, and doctor. The wife invited them to share a table and enjoy spice food.

They had a small talk as they get Alie to be on the tug team. Where the Calico Kitchen was out of comp, he could tug for boat. They would send Rocco to cook and Goushu to sing in English, even though he doesn't know what he is saying. Rocco taught him Italian songs.

The restaurant was now open, and the two chefs were Goushu and Rocco. They were the big shots.

Goushu was organizing the drag shoe to open next week with the winner getting their picture on the front marquee and a bar tab for $250. Kimmy was singing one night a week as a female. She was big hit, and Rocco took on a protective role. Goushu was a karate expert and could kick ass, but Rocco protected her. They set up queen's night and started the show.

Goushu was sad playing the piano, and Deana came in to console him. He told her he's trans. She told him she was too, and no one knew. She told him to be patient and take care of business now while he is young. She told him to do minor stuff to keep him going and she will make contact with a surgeon for hormones. "We will keep it a secret," Deana said.

Episode 13

Feathers was going to tug against Harry's Knockout. A meeting was held with all the staff at feathers combined with the new restaurant and the boat people.

Iris told Nicole, "We have one of the big Coast Guard guys to help us tug. Tony Pedoway from the Montego Bay area. His friends call him the black mongoose. He has giant arms."

Rocco said, "Are you sure he's not from Italy?"

Iris told them if they make enough money, it will pay for the whole kitchen. Rocco told them he saw the guy that might be as good as Tyler. The team consisted of Rocco, the Mongoose, Andy, Goushu, and Olga.

Iris told them, "If we win, you get three days off with pay. If we lose, you will be working for nothing for the rest of the season." Iris chose Rocco as the team captain because he was the only one that can speak to them all. Rocco told them how the team will be set up—Olga up front, Mongoose up back, the rest in the middle. He promised the Mongoose coconut shrimp with rum and told Goushu free panty hose for the next month. He also told Olga he would give her the best bottle of Russian vodka he can find and Tony Pedoway to give Tyler some knockout drops.

Iris and Nicole had a secret meeting after everyone left. Iris told Nicole if they win, they should buy the Glistening Clover down on Duval Street. She said, "It's small but we can make it work. We will buy it through a third party, and we will have the whole area under our control. No one will be told it is ours." Iris asked Nicole when Deana was coming back because the next day was the tug.

Nicole said yes to buying the bar. "We can put dancers there and water the drinks down We will talk after the tug. Let's make sure that the other team gets drunk. We will have the preparty here and work on Tyler. We can put magic in the beer, so they won't suspect anything."

BaBa started fight. He liked the roller derby queen, and they flirted with each other. Billie Joe gave them both a drink. Alie knew that Billie gave them a bad drink. Roller derby queen got pissed at Billie because she was jealous. She and Billie had a fight, and Billie pulled her hair, and some came out. The queen punched her. Rocco wanted to break it up but didn't. The other guys seemed to like it. Billie Joe recovered from the punch and jumped on the queen with her knife and cut a bunch of her hair off. Iris broke it up.

Billie Joe taunted the queen and said, "You met your match, bitch!"

The queen said, "I guess I met my match."

Goushu took the mike and sang "Strangers in the Night" and stopped all the trouble.

They all like her legs. Iris said, "Kimmy is good. We can use some new blood on our crew."

The lights went down, and everyone was dancing. Billie Joy asked Alie to dance in order to taunt the queen, and she knocked Billie Joe out. Olga stepped in to help Billie. She picked the queen up and wanted to kill her, but Rocco stepped in to get Olga under control. Roller derby saw Olga. She thought Olga was a guy and decided to rally her team for the tug. Queen told Tyler about the fight.

He said, "Olga is my friend," and he indicated to the queen to stay away from her.

Iris opened the bar to get them drunk. The people who were going to bet on Harry's Knockout wanted to change their minds, but Nicole won't let them. They all went home at two in the morning. Nicole told them all the rope pull will be at seven, and before the pull, they are having a cookout.

"That's good enough for them sail boaters," she said. "We will raise the price of the drinks. No happy hour. Tell them half is going to charity."

Nicole said, "I'm expecting big crowd will be there. All the cops can drink free. If the chief came, put him in the back and give him champagne. If the mayor comes, Iris will entertain him. She can wrap him around her finger. Treat the gays nice. Give them the good stuff to drink. They are our best customers. They will be here to see all the muscle. The rope pull is now."

The rules called for all the pullers to be wearing high heels. They had a guest judge coming named Dr. Ruth. Her job was to address the crowd and read the rules. She also quizzed them about their sex life. They also had a cheering section headed by Richard Simons. The pull started when she dropped the middle of the rope with the marker on it, and it hit the sand. It was hot from the day's sun. The pull took a full five minutes. The Feathers team won. Iris and Nicole were happy. Rocco and Goushu put together a big meal, and the party began.

Episode 14

Iris and Nicole were going to bank this money for the bad times. The new kitchen was paid for, thanks to Rocco's work. Now all they had to do was buy the Glistening Clover.

"We need a third party to purchase it. Who can we get?" asked Iris.

Nicole said, "Goushu is a good candidate. Key West needed a Chinese restaurant. It is small, and we will make it famous. He offers 65,000. He only wanted the license and location, not the good will."

They didn't want anyone else to know. They signed the papers, and a week later, they owned it. It would be a gay lipstick bar called Schaysel. It was run as a gay bar by a female named Dedra. The bar was called La Femena—an upscale bar for the rich society girls. With a dress code and a cover charge.

Iris had a female vocalist in mind called Florrie La Ponds. Iris wanted to hear her sing with Goushu. They would have chic music on Fridays and on Wednesdays. They would have broad way night. Nicole was happy at the thought of a high-class lesbian bar. They talked about Murphy, if he found out. They copied Rocco and said, "We were known as the poorest bar owners alive."

Nicole and Iris decided to have only Billie's beer and a great selection of wines, along with an expensive list of liquors. They wanted to be up and running in a week or so. They wanted Teddy Shaw for the inspector and gave him a nice cigar with a one-hundred-dollar bill wrapped around.

"If the other inspector comes, do whatever he wants you to do. Once we get open, if any bull dykes come, give them a big cover charge. They need to decorate nicely with tiffany lamps and a Steinway piano and paint the interior a pretty soft color."

Rocco and Andy painted. Iris told Rocco if he spilled one drop of paint, he would have to lick it up with his tongue. The outside also. Deana was the decorator. Daniel Murphy saw Deana went in and figured out they tricked him about Chinese bar. It would be private club, and only members were allowed in. They could let someone in and then sign them up for a dollar to keep out the rift raft. They would have a couple of private rooms. They hired a woman who did impressions of famous women such Marline Detract, with Goushu dressed up as a girl.

Nicole told Iris she was against this type of bar because they never work out, but this was different, so Nicole was happy, and Iris agreed with her. "Let's hope for a good season."

Iris sang a song. She was so happy, and Nicole told her she loved working with her. It was now the second week of October. They wanted to be open by November 1. Iris told Nicole, "We can run a very nice travel package on the yacht. The gay men have their fun. We should advertise in the big Florida cities. We can package this as a girls-only thing. We have everything ready to go."

Nicole wanted to have eighteen people, so they can have group and charge fifty thousand for boat and food. They would love Billie and Deana. They both agreed that it would work as a gold package for the lesbian girls. "We would advertise in the gay magazines only. The season is starting, and each one of the bars is ready."

They had a staff meeting on the boat. Everyone except Rocco. Iris asked them how much money they had to work with. Deana should advertise in the local gay magazine called the gentle kiss, which covers the whole eastern seaboard. The ad will cost them about seven hundred dollars. Nicole wanted Billie to be a greeter at the door, and Deana would head the boat. Nicole introduced Dedra to Billie. Dedra wanted to pick out her own staff, two pretty women for waitress and two at first to bartend. Nicole gave the approval. The dress for the staff would be a sexy but dignified uniform. The barmaids would show cleavage with skirts. Billie would wear tux top, short skirt, hose, and should look pretty. Billie was not happy with stockings. Olga would be the bouncer for the first month. Rocco gave her the instructions to be good at it. The girls had a nickname for Rocco—Unck the Hunk. The opening was on October 27.

They got a call from a group of sixteen ladies who want to fly down for fourteen days on the boat. They wanted to know if they spent an extra week, could they get a better price. Deana wanted the group, and Iris agreed on an extra week for thirty-five thousand. It was the best they can do. The leader for the group was Linda Simeron. Most of the group were from New Jersey. They flew from Newark to Key West. They got the extra two days for nothing.

Deana asked Iris about the pickup. They needed a pretty girl to pick them up, instead of Andy. Iris quizzed Deana about this. Billie had a driver's licenses, and she drove hot rods. The Rolls was different, but she could do it. She picked them up at the airport. As they exited the plane, Billie had a sign to get them into the car, but the Rolls only held half the group. They decided who will be first. Billie dropped them off and went back to get the rest of the group. Billie got the rest, and they had drinks. She told them they would like the boat.

It's hot, but when they got on the yacht, they appreciated the breeze and had lunch. They were shown to their rooms and given their itinerary. They liked Deana and Billie for their looks. They were told they were going to an exclusive club; only invited guests would be there. They got introduced to Rocco, the chef. Rocco was ready to go when he saw the girls, so Deana had to relax Rocco, so he was told they were lesbians. They were settled in and waited for dinner. Rocco made a nice veal marsala with hors d'oeuvres. He was serving and being good but still eyeing the girls.

Goushu came in and entertained them. They were told they were going to the Sychell. Two more guests were arriving two days late. They all headed out the Sychell. Deana told the girls to look good. It was semi-formal high-class club, and their membership was included in the package. Andy took them in the Rolls. Billie greeted them at the door. The girls were eying her up and down. She was cute. The club now has 35 percent members at $500 each. The rest were walk-ins. Iris couldn't wait to tell Deana. The manager came over and introduced herself as Dedra. She gave them complimentary champagne and told them they would have a show now.

The singer named Florrie was singing a ballad, and everyone was slow-dancing. She did a Marlene Dietrich song and was joined by Goushu as Marlene also. They had a debate as to who was the real Marlene and went out in the audience to dance with each girl and gave them their gift of earrings. The girls were getting drunk, and Iris was happy. And they were welcomed to Sychell, the house of women where you can be comfortable. It's the only bar one would feel comfortable in on the island.

Last call was sounded. Florrie invited them back next week for a tango contest. Andy picked them up in the Rolls. They had a special breakfast at the yacht and more entertainment. Nine fit in to the Rolls. The others got invited to a party. Deana okayed it, and the rest went back to boat. One girl was flirting with Deana.

Deana told them, "Breakfast will be waiting. Goushu will sing."

Rocco made them a great breakfast crepes set. Goushu played a Frank Sinatra song one more time. He took his wig off. They all laughed about being fooled. Goushu would take them shopping.

Episode 15

On lunch time, Deana announced to the girls that they will see a big event Friday night in front of the Feathers, with a big surprise guest called Electra. Deana introduced them to Olga, then went to a shopping trip. They were amazed at how big Olga was. Deana took them to old town. They all finished up at the bar where a lot of activity were in the works, decorating for the big tug of war between Olga and Tyler. Nicole came over to see the girls and was interested in one of them. One girl was looking back. Electra entered and was introduced to the girls. They talked. All the books were closed, but if they want to get in on it, Nicole would take the bet. They all wanted Olga to win. Billie Joe arrived to show them around for the afternoon. This freed up Nicole and Deana to make plans. They changed the rules about pulling. Five feet, there was a black line in the sand whoever was pulled over the line loses one out of three. The first to win two out of three was the champion. Olga won the first one. Tyler won the second. Each win was followed by a tie breaker. The third pull was the big one. They were very even in strength. BaBa Alie tried to keep his promise to Rocco to spike Tyler's drink, but Tyler didn't drink it. They were going to the last pull as even match. They were pulling for all they were worth, and Olga was losing. Tyler had her almost to his side of the line.

Suddenly, Olga's father, along with Martina Navatalova, showed up to encourage her to win. Olga got all excited and pulled Tyler off his feet and across the sand to her side. Tyler gave up and said, "The better person won."

Martina gave Olga an award. She made the headlines in all the gay papers, but she didn't know what gay was. She and Martina talk in Russian about being celebrities. Rocco gave her a hug and made her favorite meal, lasagna.

Episode 16

Nicole told Iris she had some friends from New York, coming down to rent the boat to go to the Turks and Cacaos. She met them on her trip up to sell her bar. They would rent the boat for about fifty thousand. They needed four days at the island. Iris needed to restore Penny to the captain's role again to get the boat there and back. She sent the Rolls to the airport to pick up guest. Andy was driving and was dressed up correctly. Deana was told to dress to the nines, in good clothing as well as the rest of the crew. They arrived at the airport around six, then to the yacht. Deana was at the boarding ramp to meet them. She asked if they would like to freshen up to have cocktails.

Deana asked them their names. They were Denise Fairmont. Husband, Randolph Fairmont. Roderick Dun. Emil Dun. They wanted to leave in the morning, but Penny was not there yet, so they were worried they'd find out Penny got arrested for being in a gambling game dressed as a girl. He had to be in front of the judge in the morning. Rocco went there and started acting as Penny's lawyer. He got arrested for contempt of court. So they sent Deana because it was judge's white head, and she had a connection. He took her to his quarters, and they flirted. And so he let Rocco and Penny go with a fine and a promise Rocco would make a bunch of cannolis paid by Iris.

Deana asked Rocco, "Can't I send you any place?" They sneaked Penny in because he was still girl and changed to man's clothing. The captain told them they had to gas up. They had a place that had clean gas, so they won't have a problem. They were heading south along the Cuban coast to the Turks. They were having brunch, so they talked about the trip. They had slip number 10 reserved because the queen was arriving. Mrs. Fairmont knew the queen was coming in.

She asked, "How long will it take to get there?"

Deana told her, "A day and a half."

They were pleased with the accommodations, and they had Japanese and Italian chef aboard. "We like fish, and the idea of Japanese and Italian are great to look forward to."

It's nine at night. Goushu was going to entertain them with singing and piano. Emil asked for a Barbara Streisand song, and Goushu sang it in Barbara's voice, and it sounded terrific. They loved it. Emil requested the song on a clear day. He sang and played it on the piano. Then he did Mrs. Marvelstein. She wowed them. So they tipped Kimmy fifty bucks. Rocco came out with the best meal presentation he has ever shown. The guests gave accolades. Deana told them they would arrive at the dock the early morning. They were told by Penny they had to clear customs. Customs and immigration came aboard, and they already knew about Rocco by way of the immigration man's cousin. The black Mongoose US Coast Guard.

Rick Belvedere was one customs guy. Deana welcomed them on the boat. They asked about Rocco. They wanted to interview him; they knew he's good. Rocco came up from the galley. Nick needed an Italian fix, so he asked Rocco to fix up something nice. Rocco made him a bucket of sauce and told him to come back later. He wanted to go drinking with him to pick up island girls where the price was low, but the price wasn't low anywhere because of the tariffs on the booze. Rocco went with them. The rest were talking and waiting for the queen's yacht to arrive, so they were listening to the ship's radio.

Roderick Dun was in the royal navy and knew the queen. Penny also knew her, but not a good thing. The day of her arrival was coming. The Duns were invited to join her on board for drinks. She addressed him by his rank, and they talked. The queen offered them a Cumber Sand "Please invite your friends to our party tonight."

Roderick told her about Rocco. She wanted to know what he cooks. "He is ten times better than the best place in England. Guess who the captain of the yacht is." He told her it's Pendleton. She and the three English women and mates were guests on board. They were told one of the activities planned for them was a turnabout contest.

"The idea," explained Deana, "is to switch roles with your mate."

One woman liked the idea for her sex life. The man got off on gender-switching roles and found out he was a transvestite, liked silk stockings, and he reacted negatively. Rock came on board, and he couldn't believe how big and beautiful the yacht is. They have a crew of cooks as big as a restaurant. Rocco was told he was in command of the kitchen. He couldn't believe he was in such a good luck situation and actually paused to think about it. He made five good dishes, with appetizers. The stewards were trying to tell Rocco he couldn't see the queen.

The head chef was laughing about Rocco being naive and helped him get an interview with the queen. The chef gave him the hat from his head. He would frame it to cherish Rocco, shed some tears, and said he would frame it. The queen sent her compliments to Rocco. The head chef got him up to the queen's deck. Rocco had his cook outfit on and was anxious to shake her hand. Rocco thanked the queen and was anxious. She thanked him for the wonderful meal. Rocco told her the facilities are great. The queen asked him to cook for the next four days. She would make him a royal cook and pay him.

Rocco couldn't believe his good luck. She asked him about Pendleton. Rocco said something derogatory, and the queen acknowledged her dislike for Pendleton. She and Rock had a conversation about him.

The queen said, "He is not really on."

And Rocco said, "Pendleton is always off."

The queen asked what he would cook tomorrow. Rocco had to think about it and won't tell her. He would be back for breakfast. He was the hero at the yacht with the rest of the gang. Rocco used the queen's words right on, and it sounded funny coming from him. He told Iris how good the galley was, and he was invited to cook for the next four days. Penny was told by Rocco that the queen said he was not on. He called Rocco a galley slave. Rocco thanked Roderick Dun for getting him on the boat. Pendleton wanted Rocco to get him in good with the queen.

Rocco said, "Okay, if you let me drive the boat."

Pendleton agreed. Rocco went to make the queen a special breakfast. Rocco's friend got him a couple of goose eggs to make a special omelet. He arrived on board the queen's yacht named *Britannia* and started to make special meal of truffle omelet. The queen's chef, named Peaches, was there to help him. Peaches was impressed with Rocco even though has no formal training. Rocco guided the rest of the kitchen crew.

Peaches said, "They will present it themselves." He had to serve the tea himself, so Rock wouldn't spill it. Rocco called the queen an old broad. He found out what not *on* means from Peaches and was trying to teach him some English ways. Rocco told him about Goushu teaching him to present food the proper way.

He told the other chef about Goushu's ability to crack him while they work together. "The chef has a little dog, a York pooch that stays in the corner. We have a pooch we call José," Rocco said. "I call him Cuddles."

The both went up to serve breakfast. The guards went to check him out again. The chef told Rocco, "Because they might think you are a mad Irish men."

Rocco told him, "I won't kill the queen. I am Italian, and I have Irish friends in Boston. Why would we want to kill the queen?"

They arrived at the queen's area. Peaches offered the queen tea and told her Rocco made her an omelet. She loved it, and they left. The queen liked her breakfast alone, so she could read the papers. Rocco said he understood her preference to be alone and to listen to opera. Rocco asked her about Penny going to the dinner dance on Wend. It will be by invitation only, printed out on a list. He got Penny on the list, and Penny thanked Rocco. Billie Joe needed some help up.

Deana told her to smile and show a little leg. "Shut up so you don't cause trouble."

Rocco had to find a suit. Pendleton's clothing almost fit him, but the pants needed to be altered. Goushu sewed his pants at the party. They asked Goushu to be the entertainment. Andy was dressed up and looking good. Rocco made up a special concoction for the queen, and Andy delivered it to the queen.

She asked "Who is this Andy?" and was told he was Rocco's assistant. She was taken by Andy's looks and says to herself, *I'm glad my husband is not here*. She asked him to pop the cork. She interviewed Penny as she got Andy to stand by. She asked Penny to fix her up with Andy and she would restore his honor. Andy was game because he never made it with an older woman. The night ended.

Episode 17

Goushu was disappointed. The queen didn't hear him sing because she was mesmerized by Andy. Iris told him to be patient. They would be there a few more days. The queen didn't like Barbara. They had a fight once. The Fairmonts asked Iris to stay one more day. Goushu brought back the answer. They would stay one more day because the queen will be their guest. They were charged eight thousand more, and they liked it. Everyone was happy. They hoped to get invited back because of Andy. The queen's steward invited them over at nine o clock and asked if they would send Andy over about seven to pick up gifts so she can be alone with him.

The party that night was informal. Andy showed up on time. The queen gave him a personal tour of the yacht. They wound up in her suite. Andy thought the queen has potential with good legs. Iris had the idea of giving the queen a present. Goushu was going to play a song, "Strangers in the Night."

Everybody was excited. The queen wanted to talk to Roderick about a commission, and Goushu was ready to entertain them. He sang a selection from Andrew Lloyd Weber after "Strangers in the Night."

The queen asked if he was a Broadway star. Rocco said he was the house queen. The queen was told what a house queen is, and she said, "Like Lady Dane."

She took her leave. Penny was trying to steal her shoes, and a guard caught him. The queen was told about Penny's actions. She said to Penny, "Are you at it again? All you had to do is ask! I had a good time, so you can have the shoes. Make sure the chef Rocco comes back, and make sure Andy comes also." She told him she would be back there in six weeks, and she wanted Rocco, so they had to make sure Rocco was there. "If you pull it off, we will restore your status. Tell the pretty blonde to send over a case of sparkling water."

She dismissed him. The queen gave Rocco an official royal guest chef award—a framed parchment proclamation of this value to the world of food.

Episode 18

The group said good-bye to the queen and headed home. On the way, the captain turned the boat over to Rocco to take it home. They were in between Cuba and Key West, and Rocco decided to go to Cuba without getting permission from the US authorities. He wanted to stop for a minute to get some cigars. The port they entered was open to foreign yachts, and they were allowed into the marina. The captain was awoken to land the boat. He thought he was in Key West.

The Cuban authorities boarded the boat to check out the papers. Rocco does not have his passport and was in trouble again. The Cubans found out he was famous chef by seeing his award from the queen, so they asked him to make a great dish aboard the yacht, and they told him he had to stay on the boat. The rest could go ashore. The captain was furious at Rocco because he knew they had broken the law and had to sneak out of here and back to the Key West. Castro found out that Olga was here and tried to keep her. Rocco was becoming the ship's lawyer, again.

Castro gave them all a state dinner to get Olga to come to his Olympic team. He knew how strong she was and that she was Alexis's sister. Rocco got the news on the boat because he couldn't go ashore with them. He promised her he would make her favorite food twice a week if she stayed with them. The Cuban leader gave them Cuban cigars to take back to Key West.

They were refueled and cleared to leave, so the captain took charge of the boat again. He knew the yacht was going to be picked up coming out of Cuba because the coast guard was always looking for rugs and boat people.

On the way to Key West, the Coast Guard caught them. The boat that found them was commanded by the Mongoose. He was surprised to see them out there, but when he found out that Rocco was driving, he wasn't surprised. They told Captain Pendleton that he would have to turn over the cigars and cook them a great meal and have it waiting when they get to Key West. They all agreed and headed home to the marina.

At the marina, the Mongoose and Rocco got into an argument over the cigars. Olga settled it by taking them to Feathers. Rock and the Mongoose made amends, and Mongoose gave Rock three out of four cigars.

Goushu was performing that evening. Nora was sitting, listening to him sing, and Rocco befriended her by buying her a glass of wine. Nora was happy to find a new friend. Rocco was finally getting used to the Conk way of life.

Iris entered at eleven o clock and greeted Nicole with a hug and saw the old lady called Nora.

She said, "I remember you in the play *Fleder Muse* I saw as a young girl." She asked her if she was Norma Bloom and invited her to the table with Billie and Deana.

Iris announced on the mike that they have a celebrity in the room, and Nora was happy to have the attention.

Kimmy sang another song, and Iris and Nora said he has good voice.

Iris said, "He is cook and very talented."

Nora said, "I really enjoyed this. I don't get a chance to get out much."

Iris told her she will have Rocco pick her up and take her back to the bar.

Rocco saw her house, which was very expensive. He told Iris about it. He told the barmaid to put Nora's drinks on his bill. She drank cognac. She was a minor celebrity attracting the gays and trans. Iris invited her to the boat Monday or Tuesday for dinner. Nora said she will be there and appreciates the company. Rocco outdid himself and made her special plate of escargot. Nora was never on a yacht before and was amazed at the accommodations. Nora told Rocco that it's good to be aboard.

Iris came to talk with Nora about the Fantasy Feast Parade. She asked Nora to be the celebrity on their float. And Nora agreed.

Episode 19

Goushu designed the float, and Rocco, Olga, and Andy built it. Goushu designed a Japanese tea garden scene. And Rocco, Olga, and Andy built it on a boat trailer to be pulled behind the Rolls. During construction, the other bars tried to get their ideas, but Rocco put beeswax on all the doorknobs to deter them. This backfired when they tried to remove it. The beeswax got all over them, and they couldn't get it off. They had to put a trailer hitch on the Rolls to pull the float, and Olga showed the welding skills that she learned at the shipyard. The float was complete, and they had a beautiful-looking float. The day of the parade was at hand, and the three of them were drinking vodka. Olga was capable of downing a lot before she gets drunk, but today, she hasn't eaten lunch, and it hit her faster than usual. Olga was driving the float and crashed into a kiosk and got something stuck under the wheels trailer. Everyone was trying to help her move it, but she took over and lifted it up by herself and put it back on the Rolls. A passerby said, "Oh, that's my macho girl."

They continued the parade and won a prize at the ceremony. A sudden tropical storm came and did a lot of damage. The roof of Nora's house got torn off, and Iris invited her to stay on the boat.

Iris sent Rocco and Olga to see if they can fix anything. Rocco told them that the house was bad, the roof was gone, and it would take a long time to fix it.

Nora was broke, and she had no insurance. She planned to sell her jewelry. Maybe Rocco can convert the house into a B&B. Iris had an idea of buying herself to convert it. Iris told her if she sells the house to them, she could live on the boat. She would have money to spend. The house was worth about seven hundred thousand. Nora said yes to the offer and put the money in the bank. She was becoming a big shot and started to sing at the bar. Nora was getting older and was anxious to do something good with her money.

Thanksgiving was coming, and Rocco told Billie to get Deana and get some ice cream at the parlor on Duval Street. Rocco wanted to do Thanksgiving. The others didn't know about this holiday. Rocco wanted a party on the boat and invited all their friends. Rocco wanted to decorate the boat for Christmas, and Deana wanted to know how much it will cost. Rocco said three thousand. Deana asked Iris. Iris knew it was a big deal. She wanted to have a buffet at the bar. She said that's too much and finally agreed to it, thinking of keeping the crew happy.

Rocco talked with Nora and told her they are preparing for Thanksgiving. Nora was happy to help with the turkey. Rocco and Nora did the Thanksgiving dinner. Billie Joe made a fruit cake. They were all in the kitchen.

The dinner was at six o'clock because Rocco wanted to help feed the poor at the mission, and they all helped him. Nora liked Rocco, and she was thinking of leaving some to Rocco. She hired the mayor of Key West to be her lawyer.

The dinner was served, and at the last minute, Joan Collins showed up, and the mood was very happy, and Iris gave her a hug, and she told Joan she was getting too pretty, and Joan told Iris she has good legs. Joan told Nora she heard about her. Rocco wanted to make a toast before they carve the turkey.

Rocco said, "I am the poorest man in the world. However, there is no one richer than me because I have you as a family. This is the true meaning of thanksgiving. Salute to everyone including Penny."

Olga carved the bird, and Nora got the first plate.

Iris was the next to speak.

She said, "We started off in England as a ragtag group. We made it to America, thanks to Penny. We are a four-star B&B, and we have a lot of money. I am truly happy to be in America to enjoy the fruit of my labor. Thank you for the chef. I hate fish and chips. Thanks Rocco."

Nora said, "In 1934, when everyone hated everyone, and I started dressing all the straights. I was a mother, and now, I am a mother. I have you."

Episode 20

Key West was in a festive mood and was decorating. All the people involved in the decorating were going to have a town meeting with the mayor. He wanted it to be the brightest Christmas ever. The mayor said, "We will have all the boats in a circle to put on their lights for world peace and happiness. Each boat will be like a float. The bar owners are to decorate according to plan."

Two weeks before Christmas, they would test the system.

All would contribute money. Rocco and Olga screwed up something, like the lights on the bar and inside, and they blew the power in that whole section.

They tried to fix it themselves, and a drag queen came in to help Rocco fix it. She was an electrician. Her name was Ms. Dazzy because she has a giant penis and drove Ms. Daisy. She got Rocco to help to tease him. The gays and trannies all teased him when they can. She showed him her breast and said she would trade for cookies. Rocco called them petunias, and Iris came to get it under control. If Nicole saw this, she'll murder Rocco.

The drag queens would do a Santa show and do a dance. Rocco said all this legs and they have something between them. He decided to get Luke involved because of the big boobs, so Luke came down to see and saw it's a gay bar.

Luke said that they were in the gay bar, and Rocco said he worked next door. Luke still wanted to see the big boobs. Rocco gave him a tour of the town to see the decorations.

Luke wanted to see Iris on board the yacht to get together with her. She told him if he kept Rocco under control, he could drink for free. Luke offered to decorate the Rolls with lights from the cigarette lighter.

Iris offered Luke a glass of wine, and they had a toast to the holidays. Iris asked Luke about his family, and he told her they're okay. Iris was a tease and never stopped with Luke.

The lights on the streets would be turned on, and they would have a bomb fire to rid the world of bad things each one would throw things in.

Luke said, "I don't know what to throw in, but I know what not to. I still remember the kiss you gave me last time."

Iris knew he was full of shit. The big drag queen with the big boobs came, and Rocco tried to get Luke to go for it. Luke knew about the gay part and was planning something to get Rocco. He paid her to get Rocco drunk, so he could get pictures. He would get Iris in bed or in on the joke on Rocco.

Episode 21

Iris called a meeting on board. They discussed mass. She told them she wanted a closed Christmas party on the upper deck. Since no one has a family there, she wanted it to be big. Rocco was assigned to make a goose dinner. He said it should be easy.

They would have a big tree to decorate. Billie was in charge of decorating inside the boat. Penny won't be there because of a trip to England to hear his sister's will and try to buy his old house back.

Rocco has to cook with a special meal for Penny to celebrate Christmas. He cooked brownies with grass in them, and the captain took them with him to England.

Penny was staying at Daniel Murphy's house. He found out that his old properties were selling for one hundred pounds.

His sister left him just enough to buy the house. He was now a knight, and he got an audience with the queen, and he told her he brought her a gift from Rocco. She was happy to hear Rocco cooked for her. She was presented with the brownies and shared them with Prince William. After she ate a couple of them, she said, "These are the best fucking brownies I ever ate."

The prince agreed. The next day, she told Pendleton to bring more brownies.

Pendleton called and told Iris he bought the house back. She said, "Good, the best thing you ever did."

Pendleton got stopped at the airport by one of the drug-sniffing dogs. The dog was sniffing him, so he ate his last cookie to hide the evidence.

He told Rocco that the queen was happy with the brownies and wanted more. Rocco said they were meant for him, not the queen. Pendleton got mad at Rocco and tried to kill him with one of the meat cleavers. Rocco told him he put mixed nuts. Rocco got busy baking more brownies for the queen. He got angry at Pendleton for putting him in the middle of this situation. Iris appeared and asked what they are fighting about. He told her that her inheritance was in the bank in England, then told her they could make his house a B&B. Iris agreed and left.

Pendleton tried to get Rocco's brownies in a diplomatic pouch and talked to the consulate who called the FBI, thinking that he was smuggling stuff.

They got to the boat to investigate, and José barked to warn Rocco about them, then José peed on their feet.

Rocco put the brownies in a cigar box inside the cigars to hide the smell of grass with the cedar scent of the box.

The English authorities were aware but thought it was fun to keep the old broad tight. They didn't intercept the import.

About the Author

Dean was born in Newark, New Jersey to a humorist mom of English descent. On the very day she got her United States driver's license, she backed into a patrol car. When the police officer got to her window she said so sorry constable I miss calculated you know your steering wheels are on the wrong side. Dean laughed and just had to write it down. From that moment on, he knew that writing was exciting and fun.

CPSIA information can be obtained at www.ICGtesting.com
Printed in the USA
BVOW08s0504230715

409776BV00001BA/13/P